Other Mark Daniel titles published by Armada

On the Spot
MacGyuer on Ice

Mark Daniel

In a Spin

An Armada Original

In a Spin was first published in the
UK in Armada in 1988

Armada is an imprint of the Children's Division,
part of the Collins Publishing Group
8 Grafton Street, London W1X 3LA

Printed and bound in Great Britain by
William Collins Sons & Co. Ltd, Glasgow

"So," Mrs Crispin smoothed her silk skirt over her thighs with long spangled fingers, "Let's have a decision. Film or theatre?"

"Theatre," Katie Crispin declared.

"Now, now, Katie," her mother smiled indulgently. She leaned back and sipped tea from a pink and gold cup. "It's Paul's birthday treat. He must decide. You've had your birthday."

"Oh, all right," Katie shrugged ungraciously. She snatched a crumpet as though stealing it. "But Paul's going to want to see some totally babyish film and it'll be really boring for everyone else. I want to go to the theatre." Her white teeth crunched into the crumpet. Melted butter made her chin gleam.

"Yes, well. It's up to Paul."

"Paul can't decide anything. You know that."

Paul Crispin, the subject of their conversation, sat glum and silent on the window-seat and stared at his knees. He was a fair, slightly chubby boy with very pink cheeks. He would be thirteen on Saturday. Right now all he wanted was to escape from his mother's fussing and Katie's constant mockery. Sitting in the drawing-room and being expected to talk made him feel embarrassed. He longed to be alone down by the stream with Flurry, his black and white spaniel. He loved the sound of the winking brown water, the smell of rotting leaves, the occasional splash and flash of silver as a trout leaped . . .

"Paul!" his mother was calling, exasperated, "Oh, for goodness sake, kick him, Katie."

Paul sat up and cast a warning glance at his sister. She was a year older and two inches taller than he, but had recently developed the habit of shrieking very loudly whenever he hit back. "Sorry," he said. "What?"

"Have you decided what to see on Saturday?"

"Um, a film, please," Paul replied. "Something exciting. *Cantiger's Will.*"

Katie groaned. Paul had expected that. Whatever he had said, she would have groaned. "Oh, no!" she wailed, "I told you, Mummy. It's all ships and treasure and violence and stupid things like that. Chloe Mather saw it and she says it's rubbish."

Paul shrugged. "Well, lots of boys at school have seen it and they thought it was great."

"They would," Katie sneered. "I think it's really selfish of you. I mean, we've all got to see this, not just you. You don't think about that, do you, Paul?"

Paul shrugged again. He refrained from reminding her that, on her birthday, he had had to sit for three hours at the Coliseum watching men in tights and women dressed as confectionery prinking about the stage.

"Can we go skating, Mummy?" Katie licked buttery fingers. "It's on the way, isn't it? Richmond, I mean."

"I suppose . . . Yes, I suppose we could. I used to live at Richmond, you know. Lovely big house. I haven't skated for years . . ."

"We went from school. I was really good at it."

"You've never been skating, have you, Paul?"

"Er, no." Paul shook his head.

"Oh, Paul won't like it," Katie predicted with satisfaction. "He'll be useless. I bet he spends all the time on his silly fat bottom."

"Now, now, Katie. You never know, Paul may turn out to be very good at it. Stranger things have happened. He's got much better balance than you, actually."

"Can I go now?" Paul asked eagerly, then checked himself. "I mean – well, I'd like . . ."

"Of course, darling," his mother stood to rearrange a

flower display in the corner. "Off you go. We'll call you when it's supper-time."

Paul jumped up. He almost trotted from the room. A moment later, his footfalls sounded like a drum-roll on the stairs. Katie's eyes rolled heavenward. "Extraordinary brat," she announced.

The roots of a pollarded crack willow gripped at the riverbank as though afraid of falling into the sky. Beneath, in the reflection of its spiky branches, a trout lay. Its body waved very slowly in the stream, a vague glimmer of gold like the light of a taxi reflected in a wet pavement.

Paul held Flurry's collar tight and tried to stay still, though the midges bobbed around his face and ears and he longed to brush them away. He released the spaniel to snuffle along the bank, then stood and strolled downstream.

Now he could see the long white house clearly above him on his left, which meant that anyone standing at the bow-windows could see him too. He preferred the shady hidden places along the hundred yard stretch, the places where he could be alone with his thoughts.

It wasn't that he disliked his family or indeed his teachers and contemporaries at school. It was just that they pried too much, demanded of him too many responses, expected him to behave in this way or that, whilst he was shy and liked best to read, to keep his diary, to walk alone. Their constant interruptions and interventions made him so tense that at times he wanted to lash out, and then he would say things that he did not mean simply in order to drive them away.

The Crispins had moved to Wraysbury five years ago; when Paul's father, a chartered accountant, had left private practice to take up a job with a big oil firm in London. Before that, they had lived in a thatched cottage in the Hampshire countryside. He missed the long walks, the views of open country, the ability to escape people completely.

"Paul!" the call from above made him jump. The French windows swung outward. Paul's father strolled out onto the lawn, a glass of gin and tonic in his hand, and trotted down the steep grassy slope. He wore a blue cardigan and a Panama hat. He was a young-looking forty-five with slicked back dark blonde hair. He had recently grown a paler moustache which made him look older.

Paul crossed the little footbridge to meet him.

"Hello, son," his father smiled. He had a good smile. Paul and he used to spend a lot of time together. Now Mr Crispin was always busy.

"Hello, Dad."

"Having fun down here?" Mr Crispin looked around and sniffed deeply.

"Yup."

"Not brought a rod down with you?"

"No. Not tonight. No time. Anyhow, I just wanted to – you know."

"Just have a stroll, eh? Hm. Yes. Quite so. Anyhow, it's time for supper. We must be getting in." He put an arm around Paul's shoulder and together they turned back towards the house. "Good day at school?" Tony Crispin asked.

"OK. You?"

"Busy, very busy. Still."

"Are you coming to London with us on Saturday?"

"Saturday, um, oh, no. No, sorry, I'd love to, but I'm going to have homework to do. You know. Gather you're going to see a film."

"Yes," said Paul glumly. He preferred outings when his father came too. They were easier. "And skating."

"You wanted to go skating?"

"No. Katie."

"Daft occupation, slithering about on ice. How are you getting on at games?"

"All right, I suppose," Paul shrugged.

"Good, good. Very important, games. 'Specially team games. I was a very keen footballer, you know; netball, ping-pong, boxing, rugger, everything. Important to be fit, you know. Learn to develop the winning instinct. Lot of people out there ready to compete with you. You have to be tough if you're to get on. I had to learn that. You, now, you've had a lot of advantages, but that can be a disadvantage too, you know. Too easy to grow soft, you know." He pushed open the French windows. "Well!" he cried, "Here we are!"

"Eugh!" Katie grimaced and dropped her spoon back in the soup-bowl. "I'm not going to sit next to *him*! I bet he's all filthy and smells of that stinking river."

"That's enough, Katie," her father sang, "Paul's going to wash before supper, aren't you, Paul?"

"Yes," Paul mumbled, "Just a minute. Sorry."

"There," Mr Crispin sat at the head of the table. He rubbed his hands together before plucking up his napkin. "Mmm, smells good. This is what I like, eh? All the family together at suppertime? Marvellous."

* * *

Gabriella Lombardi held her daughter's hand very tightly as they crossed Battersea Park Road. Someone wolf-whistled on the pavement behind them. She paid no attention.

You could understand why they whistled. She had less

money, perhaps, than many of the young women who jostled past her on the pavement in shapeless floral cotton-prints, but she had a sense of style. She was slim and fit. Her long brown hair was swept back off her face and bound at the nape of her neck so that it burst over her left shoulder. Her jeans were clean and well-cut. Her white silk skirt and black leather jacket were expensive, old, but well cared for. She carried herself like a beautiful woman and therefore appeared to be one. She was perhaps thirty, thirty-one.

Her daughter Anna was eleven. She too wore jeans, and a pressed pink shirt. Gabriella guided her through the crowds of passers-by into the greengrocer's.

Gabriella had always enjoyed shopping in Italy, but here it had become a penance. The pavements seemed harder, the other shoppers more hostile, the shop assistants unhelpful or downright rude.

Now her expert eye scanned the rows of potatoes, carrots, broccoli, tomatoes. Anna was selecting small new potatoes while Gabriella collected a head of celery and some peaches. Then she noticed the melons. Anna liked melons and they were cheaper than usual. It would be a nice little treat. She picked one up, sniffed it, lightly squeezed it between finger and thumb. Under-ripe. She put it down and picked up another.

"'Ere, you!" the voice behind her made her start. "What do you think you're doin'?"

She turned, eyebrows raised. A little round man with thin grizzled hair and a grubby apron pointed at the melon in her hand. His lower lip twisted and trembled in outrage.

"I am looking for a melon," Gabriella explained, "I want to buy one."

"Well, you can't touch the merchandise and put things

back. It's unhygienic. *And*," the man grabbed the fruit from her hand, "it ruins them for other customers. Don't know what they do where you come from, but here, you want a melon, you take a melon, right?"

"But you are stupid!" Gabriella cried more in astonishment than indignation. "How is possible to buy a melon without to touch it? In England perhaps you eat the skins of melons? I do not want to spend money on bad small not mature melons."

"Oh, stupid is it?" the grocer barked. "Well, let me tell you, young lady – and you," he pointed at Anna, "what do you think you're doing? You take the potatoes on top just like anybody else. Pernickety foreigners," he appealed to the other customers, "what about everyone else, eh? You can just go back to wherever you came from and . . ."

Gabriella had taken two deep breaths. She now released them with a deluge of English and Italian words in which a few grand adjectives purled and smacked like giant boulders. The other shoppers turned, some shocked, some admiring, some pretending to be deaf. The shopkeeper took two steps backward and tried to interrupt. It was futile.

At last, Gabriella had to draw breath. Anna had taken her hand and nodded agreement throughout the outburst. Now, at the door, she turned back and announced to the startled shopkeeper, "And your grandfather too!"

Gabriella giggled.

Their shopping at last completed, they trudged wearily back to Wandsworth High Road. They lived in one of four squat, square concrete blocks named the Robilliard Estate. Once the doors and balconies had gleamed, fresh-painted green, red, blue. Now the paint was scuffed and scored. Graffiti staggered along every walkway.

Gabriella and Anna clattered up the staircases to the fifth floor. The flat consisted of five rooms; a sitting-room which led on to the veranda, Gabriella's and Anna's bedrooms, a little shoebox kitchen and a bathroom. It was spotlessly clean.

The sitting-room doubled as Gabriella's studio. It was sparsely furnished in black and silver – a black lacquer table and three black vinyl chairs, all with chrome legs, black formica units on which the television and the old stereo system rested, a simple steel bookcase along one wall.

The only pictures on the walls were Gabriella's own photographs – a picture of Anna dressed as a clown for Notting Hill Carnival, portraits of tramps and partygoers, punks and peers – the colourful eccentrics of London. Occasionally she sold these pictures to foreign magazines and newspapers. She earned perhaps a third of her small income in this way. She earned the rest by cleaning the flats of well-heeled young people who worked in the city. Twice a year, too, she did fashion drawings for the collections of less proficient college-friends who had become designers.

Gabriella had been an art student in Milan and then at Chelsea in the mid-seventies. She had met and married Anna's father, Nico Taylor, when she was just twenty. Three years later, Nico had joined a religious cult and disappeared to a commune in Nepal, leaving Gabriella with a six month old child. He had never been seen or heard of since.

Gabriella had rebelled from her parents by leaving her home in the first instance. Although they had made it clear that she could return to Veneto whenever she wanted, she would not concede defeat. Once a year, she accepted two return tickets to Padua from her father, the owner of a small chain of bridal shops, but otherwise she was resolutely independent. There had been many crises, many occasions on which she had looked at the telephone and licked her lips and thought how easy it would be to ask her father's help. Somehow she had resisted. The cost, she knew, would be too great. Somehow she and Anna had survived.

Together now they emptied the carrier-bags. Gabriella started to prepare supper – risotto, cheese with olive oil, and peaches – while Anna sat at the sitting-room table and scanned the television column in the newspaper.

"Oh, Gabi," she called suddenly. "*C'e Torvill e Dean alla televisione 'sta sera.*"

"English," Gabriella corrected. The house rule ordained Italian in the morning, English at night.

"Oofa!" Anna sighed, "Torvill and Dean are on the television tonight. Please can I watch them?"

"What time?"

"Ten past nine."

"All right," Gabriella smiled, "But only if you are washed and changed into your pyjamas in ten minutes from now, OK?"

"OK," Anna leaped from her chair and ran for the bathroom, "*Grazie, mama,*" she called.

"English!" Gabriella shouted back, and grinned.

Since she had first seen skating on television, Anna had been hooked. Posters of Katherina Witt, Robin Cousins and Torvill and Dean hung on her bedroom walls. She watched every figure-skating and ice-dance championship on television, but she had only twice been skating herself. The cost of the trip to the rink, the admission fee and the hire of skates was too high. She did not complain, but her love of skating remained unabated.

That night after dinner, she sat cross-legged on a cushion on the floor and bounced up and down with excitement as the news came to an end and a fanfare of trumpets announced the European Ice Dance Championships from Helsinki.

Gabriella worked at her desk arranging her latest batches of photographs, polaroids and xeroxes into piles. Occasionally, she glanced up. Anna was wholly engrossed.

At last, Jayne Torvill and Christopher Dean glid on to the ice, dressed all in gold. "*Guarda*, Gabi, *guarda*! Look!" Anna gasped.

Gabriella laid down her papers, pushed back her chair and extended her legs. She watched the *Barnum* routine with increasing admiration and astonishment. "*Sono bravissimi*," Anna breathed. Her voice was husky. "*Sono bravissimi* . . ."

Her mother glanced sharply over at her. Tears streamed from Anna's eyes and dripped from her jawbone. She made no attempt to wipe them away but stared through the mist at the action replays.

"Anna?" Gabriella got up from her chair and in two crouching strides was by her daughter's side. "What's the matter?" she asked gently.

Anna shook her head. Hot tears splashed onto Gabriella's hand. She put an arm around Anna's shoulders and pulled her towards her, but the little girl's lower lip trembled and her shoulders shook. She wrenched free of her mother's embrace. With a little high-pitched whimper, she leaped up and ran from the room.

Gabriella stood, switched off the television and walked slowly, wearily back to her desk. This was no mere childish craze, she thought. Somehow, something had to be done.

* * *

"Oh, it's years since I've done this," Mrs Crispin tittered as she laced up her boots. "I'm sure I'll fall flat on my face as soon as I get on the ice."

"So will Paul," said Katie, "you just wait and see."

"And I suppose you're the Olympic gold medallist," Paul taunted, "I can't wait to see you."

"I'm not that good," said Katie quickly, "I never said I was. I've only done it once *actually*. Anyone can fall over, but I bet you're worse than I am, that's all."

"Hush," Mrs Crispin stood and teetered uncertainly on her skates. She propped herself up on the steel lockers. "Ooh, my ankles aren't strong enough for this. You two ready?"

"Yup," Katie stood.

"Yes," Paul sighed. He really did not want to skate. He was quite looking forward to tea, and the film sounded as if it would be fun but his idea of a treat would have been for everyone else to have gone up to London leaving him at home.

They hobbled along the carpeted corridor to the double doors of the rink. It was a Saturday afternoon in the holidays. The place was packed. Below them, a hundred or more people circled the ice. Some hurtled at breakneck speed into the barriers; some skated like Germans, very seriously, hands linked behind their backs, heads bowed; some clung to the edge, teetering like tight-rope walkers; a very few glid with enviable confidence near the centre.

Everyone moved anti-clockwise save three boys, a year, perhaps two, older than Paul, who seemed to think it funny to charge across the rink from barrier to barrier. They wore denim jackets and moleskin trousers and the short sleek hair of rodents.

Paul took all this in and breathed in very deeply. At the

bottom of the ramp, his mother and Katie had already ventured on to the ice.

"Come on, babykins!" Katie yelled, "You can do it!" She pushed herself away from the barrier and tottered, leaning forward for a few quick steps to another barrier close at hand. "See?" she chortled, absurdly pleased with herself, "It's peasy!"

Paul stepped on to the ice. He took one step forward and instantly felt his right foot slipping away from him. He had to bring his left foot up fast, then his right foot again, his left, then his right, each trying to catch up with the other. At last he lunged forward and grabbed the barrier just in time. He pulled himself upright and wiped the hair from his eyes.

"Oh, very graceful!" Katie clapped.

Paul scowled. He set off very sedately, his right hand fluttering just above the barrier. Occasionally he rowed himself along or stopped to support himself before he fell. Behind him, though he did not see her, Katie did much the same, though she tried hard to look confident and carefree. Mrs Crispin brought up the rear, pulling herself along hand over hand. They completed two circuits like that without any mishaps.

"You're meant to leave the side!" Katie called to her younger brother. She rapidly left it herself in order to overtake him.

"I know," Paul said, exasperated. "Just shut up, will you?"

He pushed himself away from the barrier and moved tentatively forward. At first, he seemed to be going smoothly, though he had to lean a long way forward. Then a girl in green flashed by. He raised a hand, overbalanced and flapped frantically as though to take off. His skates flew up. The rest of him dropped down. He landed square on his bottom. "Damn," he muttered.

Katie, still preening close to the side, hooted with laughter. "Look, Mummy, look. I told you!" she shrilled, "Leaves the side for a second and crash!"

One of the suede-headed youths hurtled past him just a foot away, and slammed into the barrier. "Nice one, kid!" he jeered in a clogged alto, "Let's have another one."

Heat prickled in Paul's cheeks. He pulled himself to his feet and again pushed forward, but, in his impatience and anger, he had not waited to recover his balance. This time, his landing made his brains clatter. His teeth clunked shut.

Katie's laughter rang in the vaults of the ceiling and made the ice sizzle. Another of the youths joined his friend. "'Allo. See you got an 'andicapped one 'ere. This should be funny. Need an 'and, mate?"

Paul ignored him. He shook his head quickly and got to his feet. Teeth gritted, he made his way to the side. His brain was very hot.

"Giving up already?" Katie skated by, arms extended, like a seagull on its maiden flight, "Cowardy cowardy cust . . ."

Her jaw dropped. Her eyes widened. Her hair spurted up. She squeaked. Her right hand clawed in vain for the barrier as her skate-blades crossed. Her fingers clasped the fabric at a passing skater's elbow. For a second or two she was dragged keening along, then she went down like a puppet when the strings are cut.

"Oh, very funny!" she spat through her hair as at last she pulled herself up. "As it happens, it wasn't my fault, *actually*. It was that man in red . . ."

Paul did not hear her. He hardly knew that she was there. If she heard laughter, it was not his but that of her former allies. Paul just frowned intently and watched the skaters behind her. He noted the way in which they pushed outward with their skates in order to increase their centres of gravity. He noticed the little back kicks, the almost upright stances . . .

"Are you okay, Paul?" his mother dragged herself from the ice and sagged into a chair.

He did not hear her either. Still frowning, he pushed himself out onto the ice again.

He had picked out a young couple as the best skaters on the rink. He waited until they passed, then dropped in behind them. He followed, his eyes fixed upon their skates. This time, he stood straight and allowed the ice to do the work for him rather than trying to run. It worked. Suddenly he discovered that, although his limbs moved slower, he actually moved more than twice as fast.

He made perhaps twenty circuits of the rink like that, conscious of nothing but the rhythm of his strides. Occasionally he had to jink to one side to avoid fallers. Once or twice he nearly fell himself.

"Paul!" his mother called, "We're just going up for a cup of tea. You coming?"

He shook his head irritably and kept going.

Another twenty circuits, and another, concentrating now on turning as smoothly and effectively as the couple that he followed.

Suddenly it felt good. He no longer even thought of falling but merely of perfecting his balance and obtaining the maximum volition from every movement. His models left the rink. Paul hardly noticed.

"Paul!"

"Paul, will you come here at once!" his mother's voice rapped at the walls.

Paul shook his head irritably. A pretty girl in pink satin trousers grasped his arm. "I think you're wanted," she smiled and pointed.

He nodded, sighed. He had enjoyed that strange hypnotic state. He had been alone there, yet his mind and his body had been active. Shaken from it now, he realized that he was cold and that his ankles hurt. He wanted to be back in that private world in which he had moved so fluently and painlessly.

He stepped neatly on to the ramp at the side of the rink.

"Oh, very flash!" Katie jeered, "You're seriously mad, you know. We were calling and calling and all you did was go round and round in circles like some sort of total idiot. Quite mad."

"Hmph," Paul sighed.

"You were going quite nicely there, darling," his mother said briskly. "Well, come on. We've got to get going. Get those skates off quickly and we'll be on our way."

Paul found it difficult and uncomfortable to walk off the ice. He hobbled painfully to the changing-room feeling, he thought, as a penguin or a swan must feel out of water, a clumsy, ungainly creature out of its element. He slumped down on the bench and unlaced his boots.

"Come on," said his mother, "I'll give you a hand." She bent and grasped each end of the right blade. "Not much wonder that you're stiff . . . Paul!" she gasped as the boot came off, "What have you done to yourself?" She pulled quickly at the other boot. "Take those socks off now."

Paul looked wearily down. There were large brown patches at the ankles and the toes of his green socks. Something cold trickled down his right instep.

He plucked at the sock. Oily blood stained his ankle.

The wool stuck to his toes. He winced as he tugged it free. It had been glued to his toes with dried blood. The first two toes and the little toe of both feet were caked with almost black blood and strands of wool. Both ankles were rubbed raw.

"I said he was mad, didn't I?" said Katie, "Eugh! It's disgusting! I think I'm going to be sick."

"Idiot," Paul's mother smiled at him with rare affection, "does it hurt?"

Paul shook his head. "Nope."

"Well, wash them quickly. We'll buy you some plasters and some new socks on the way. You are a twit."

"Yup," Paul grinned, "But I think I can skate now."

"Yes, it looked very good. I was impressed."

"I wasn't," Katie said sulkily. "He just went round and round in circles. I mean, anyone can do that. 'S easy."

"Oh, do shut up, Katie," Mrs Crispin sighed. "You can be very boring. Hurry up, Paul. We must get up to town and look for your present."

"Mum," Paul said quietly as Mrs Crispin steered the Maestro on to Putney Bridge.

"Mmm?"

"Um – you know my birthday present?"

"Yes."

"Do you think . . .? Well, I mean, I think I know what it's going to be . . ."

"Do you now? Well, you may be right. Of course, you may not be getting a present at all."

"No," he laughed nervously, "Well, but if I am, I mean . . . There's something I'd like more, if I can. If it's not too expensive . . ."

"What is it?" his mother laughed. "Come on, let's have it."

"Skates," he said, "and boots. I asked at Richmond," he gabbled, "and they said a hundred and twenty pounds for boots and perhaps eighty for a set of blades and . . ."

"And?"

"And a season ticket is about twenty five pounds."

"You, skating?" Katie struck her forehead with the heel of her hand, "I don't believe it! You're barmy, you are!"

"Yes," Mrs Crispin said decisively, "All right, darling. I don't see why not. I never did like those stupid computer things anyhow."

Gabriella Lombardi glanced quickly at her watch as she ducked out of the rain into the auction-hall. She had dropped Anna off at school just ten minutes before. She must be at a merchant banker's flat in Church Street, Chelsea, in two hours.

The auction took place every fortnight. This was the cheapest place at which to buy household goods. Here at one time or another she had bought her old Hoover, her wooden salad-bowls, duvets, rugs, trinkets for Anna and most of the china and glass in her flat. As for the rest, she merely had to sit on her hands and gnash her teeth as objects that she desired went for next to nothing.

Today she was looking for a kettle (she had been heating water in a saucepan for weeks) and, perhaps, some books for Anna, already an insatiable reader.

". . . Lot 26, one Morphy Richards electric kettle. In working order? In working order. Who'll start me at five? Five pounds . . .? Four, then . . ."

Gabriella scurried over to join the ring of people around the auctioneer. A dealer started the bidding at fifty pence. A hawk-faced woman took it up to three pounds. The dealer dropped out. Gabriella only had to bid once. She sighed with relief when the hammer fell at £3.50.

A box of lace trimmings and embroidered silk came six lots later. Gabriella estimated that she had "saved" two pounds fifty on the kettle and that, at a pinch, she could just afford a further four pounds. To her astonishment and delight, the box was knocked down to her for five pounds.

She put the kettle on top of the fabrics, picked up the box and turned towards the door.

". . . Lot 36, two pairs of ice-skates, one adult, one child's. Not bad nick, with guards. What are guards, George? Oh, right. Right, who'd like to do a bit of skating, then? Any budding Torvill and Deans out there? Who'll give me ten pounds?"

Gabriella dropped the box on the table and rushed back to the ring of spectators and would-be buyers. "Excuse me," she shouldered through, "Excuse me." At the front, she reached up and tugged at the auctioneer's jacket. Her lips were drawn back in a desperate grin of anxiety. "What size?" she pleaded.

"Five pounds, five-fifty? Five-fifty. Six?" He turned with a testy frown. "What, miss?"

"What size? The *skates*," she pointed, "What size are they please?"

"I dunno," he shrugged and turned back to the room. "Six pounds. I have six pounds. Six-fifty. Seven . . ."

A little squeak seeped from Gabriella's lips. She darted into the centre of the ring. She seized the smaller pair of skates from the bent old man in overalls who held them up.

"'Ere," he yapped, "What you doin'?"

With trembling hands, she fumbled at the tongue of one boot and squinted inside.

". . . nine, nine-fifty, ten? Ten. Ten-fifty, eleven. No? Eleven pounds. All done at eleven pounds?"

"No!" Gabriella squawked like a scared parrot. "Twelve!"

Gabriella snatched the other pair of skates and glanced quickly inside. "Thirteen!" she yelped.

The audience tittered. "It is with you, miss," the auctioneer said smoothly. "I will not ruin you. Twelve pounds, then. I have twelve pounds. All done?" The hammer rapped. "Mrs . . .? Mrs Lombody."

Gabriella clutched the skates to her chest and muttered a fervent prayer of thanks.

Only now did she have an opportunity to examine her purchases. The boots were of soft leather, probably buckskin, which had once been white on the outside but was now smoky with age. She pulled off the guards. The steel blades gleamed. She examined the edges. Aside from a few tiny hairline scratches, they were sheer and unmarked. There was no trace of rust, no nicks.

Only now too did she have time to reflect that she did not possess twelve pounds. After buying the kettle and the fabric, she had just four pounds and some loose change left in her purse. She would receive seven pounds for her two hours' work this morning, but that would have to pay for transport and for provisions for the next two days.

She calculated swiftly. There was tea, coffee, parmesan, home-made beef broth, pasta, rice and apples at home. She could open tins of tuna and ham for Anna's lunches. She had to travel to work today and on Saturday . . .

She sighed and turned towards the dealers in the corner. "Excuse me," she said, hating their marble eyes and their coarse hands. "I have this kettle . . ." she took a deep breath, "and all this *stoffa* – material. What will you give me, please?"

"I don't like always eating soup," Anna pouted. "Always soup and salad. Can't we have some chicken? Fish or *bollito* or something? It's boring!"

"Yes, well," Gabriella sprinkled grated parmesan over her own bowl, "I haven't got very much money this week. Anyhow, it's good for you. Just eat it up and don't break my boxes, OK?

"We must go to bed early tonight," she said. "I am going to see if I can find more work, and you are looking a little tired."

"I'm not," said Anna. She shoved her half-full bowl away from her.

"Well, you seem very bad-tempered to me." Gabriella ladled more broth into the bowl. "A good night's sleep will do you good."

"I'm not bad-tempered," the corners of Anna's lips twitched downward, "just fed up with always eating the same food."

"Yes, well. If you go to bed early, you might find a little surprise. And I don't want to hear any more about food. Most of the children round here are just eating greasy horrible food. You are lucky, so shut up." She pushed the bowl towards Anna. Anna pushed it petulantly back. "OK," Gabriella stood, "if you've finished supper, it's time for bed. Off you go."

"No!" Anna hit the table with her fist. The light died in her little black eyes. The colour bloomed in her cheeks. "I don't like you," she announced. Her fists opened and shut by her side, "You are horrible!" Tears sprang to the young girl's eyes. She stamped. "You don't care for me. You can keep your horrible food. I would like to be like the other children. At least they eat different things every night. And another thing, you go out sometimes and eat in restaurants and leave me here – you just don't care for me at all."

"Quite right," Gabriella opened Anna's bedroom door and pushed her in. "Nobody cares for you. Into your pyjamas quickly and off to do-do like a little baby. Come along."

She slammed the door in Gabriella's face. Gabriella whistled as she strolled back to the kitchen. Behind her, the bed-springs squeaked and the groaning, whimpering and sobbing continued.

Gabriella sat once again at the table and drank her soup. The noises from next door had died down now. Anna padded about her room. Occasionally she sniffed. Otherwise there was only the snuffling of the wind at the window, the distant tide of the traffic far below.

Gabriella stretched. She got up and poured herself a glass of red wine from a bottle which a designer friend had given her a week ago.

She waited.

She had borrowed some whitener this morning from one of her employers, a keen cricketer, and had spent two hours washing the boots, feeding the leather and restoring them to their original brilliance. They stood now amidst Anna's other shoes on the floor of her wardrobe.

The door swung open. "Mama?" Anna's voice creaked like an old door.

"Mmm?" Gabriella turned with a casual smile.

"They . . ." Anna gulped, "They are mine?"

Gabriella pretended to consider, then, "Yes, I think so."

The tears welled and spilled again. "I'm sorry," she

murmured. She reached forward and took two rapid, uncertain steps towards her mother. She had forgotten that she was wearing skates, but Gabriella was already on her knees, arms extended, to catch her as she fell. "I'm sorry," she sobbed in Gabriella's ear.

Gabriella drew back and smiled. "They fit?"

Anna nodded.

"Good. Well, if you want to be able to use them, it's going to mean lots of soup. All right?"

Anna nodded again. Her red eyes sparkled. She grinned. "All right," she croaked. "Thank you, Gabi."

"That's all right," Gabriella wiped her own eyes impatiently. "Now, off to bed with you, *subito*."

When, ten minutes later, she entered Anna's room to kiss her good-night, she found her already asleep. She raised the blankets. As she had expected, Anna had not removed the skates.

Gabriella grinned. Very gently, she removed them, replaced the guards and laid them on the pillow beside Anna's head.

She returned to her desk in the sitting-room. She had sums to do.

* * *

Chalk tapped and squeaked on the blackboard. Kass's voice rose and fell like that of the man who reads the football announcements. Outside on the lawn, a blackbird hopped. Occasionally it stopped to stab at the lawn which gleamed under a slick of rain. Wormcasts caught the sunlight. Paul glanced surreptitiously at his watch. Three o'clock. Just three hours now.

Skating. It had all snowballed so fast. He had started with five half-hour lessons, then five more. He had shown aptitude, and Mrs Mottistone, his teacher, had encouraged him to work through the grades. The basic edges – forward outside, backward outside, forward inside and – the novelty – backward inside, had proved astonishingly easy. Then came crossovers, the three jump, the selko, the upright spin. He had gone up for his Preliminary figures-and-free more as a joke than anything else. He had passed. Immediately, almost inevitably, he had found himself working towards the Bronze.

Well, as Mrs Mottistone had explained to a delighted June Crispin, it would have been silly not to. The Bronze figure test was to all intents and purposes the same as the prelim, except that this time he would have to change edge on a figure of eight rather than skating in circles, and the tracings – the patterns left by the skates on the ice – were a little more important. The free test too was little more than a sophisticated version of the prelim, but this time, for the first time, he would be skating to music.

Mrs Crispin had been defiantly thrilled. Of course, she had enthused – Mrs Mottistone was to do whatever she thought best. Just send in the bills.

His father had displayed the very opposite attitude.

"Skates?" he had howled on that first night when they had returned from London with Paul's chosen birthday present. "You bought my son *skates*? Dear God, what were you thinking of? I mean, for God's sake, what good does skating do? Tell me that."

"It gives poise and self-discipline," Mrs Crispin had answered briskly, "and it keeps you fit."

"What does the boy need poise for, for heaven's sake? I'm poised enough, aren't I, and I never needed to go poodle-faking around on the ice. And as for being fit, what's wrong with football, hmm? What's wrong with cricket, tennis? Normal sports for normal people. I mean, who do you know? – who do you know? – just name me one person you know who goes skating."

"I don't," Mrs Crispin had shrugged, "but I don't know anyone who goes ballooning either, or deep-sea diving. It doesn't mean I wouldn't let Paul do it if he wanted to. It's an interest, that's all, and I think that Paul could be really quite good, and that's all there is to it."

"Nine days' flamin' wonder, more like," Tony Crispin had shaken his head, despairing. "You just wait. Two months from now, and a hundred and eighty pounds' worth of skates will be gathering dust in the wardrobe, just you wait and see. And what about the computer? The idea was that a computer would improve his schoolwork. Skating is hardly going to do much for his French or Maths, is it?"

The battle had continued on and off ever since then. Somehow, it seemed, Paul's decision to take up skating had crystallized his parents' differences. Mrs Crispin saw herself as defending sensitivity, beauty, depth of feeling, the standards that she had known before marrying. Mr Crispin saw himself as protecting his son by asserting principles of manliness, industry and team-spirit.

Paul kept well clear of their bickering. Had they shown any real interest in his training sessions, they would have learned that elegance was attained neither by posing nor by dressing up and that hard work and physical toughness did not of their nature preclude grace or sensitivity. Day after day, Paul returned with aches in every muscle and bruises on every limb . . .

The trouble with skating, Paul had discovered, was that just as Bronze led to Inter-Silver, so each new element or figure learnt opened the door to another. No sooner had he mastered three-turns than he realized that, with a little effort, he could also master Mohawks. No sooner had he perfected Mohawks than some enviably adept and elegant skater sped past him doing cross-rolls and Paul knew that, with practice, he could do them too.

Suddenly, skating had become an obsession. Everything else – school, homework, meals, family holidays – was merely an interruption to his progress on ice. It had happened without his noticing. One day, skating had been a enjoyable if taxing hobby; the next, he woke up with toe-loops on his mind, sat at his desk staring at the wall, sorting out the faults in his change-foot sit-spin and kicked off the duvet at night as, in his dreams, he practised axels.

So absorbing was each new challenge that somehow he did not mind getting up at six o'clock every morning of the holidays in order to catch the Richmond train. He practised from anything from four to six hours daily. Mrs Crispin had waged a long and bitter battle for him to be a day-boarder at Springhill, the direct-grant school near Datchet. Mr Crispin had wanted him to board full-time. She had won. Mrs Mottistone was therefore able to arrange "patches" at the rink around his school-hours.

The opposition, however, from his father, from Katie and from his schoolfellows, had remained constant. By now, Paul was used to being called "pansy" and to seeing the other boys parodying jumps and spins whenever he passed. Katie, now a blasé sixteen-year-old who talked of nothing but public-schoolboys and parties, introduced him to her snobbish friends as "Little Paulie. He's a bit – peculiar, shall we say?"

But Paul was certainly no longer little. He was, if anything, tall for his fifteen years. Where once he had been plump, now he was lean. Puppy fat had turned to muscle. He no longer reacted to such jibes either. Skating had given him more than a preoccupation; it had given him a club. Although his fellow-skaters rarely exchanged more than a nod and a few words, they were his friends. They shared with him a passion and a dedication. From the youngest – some were only eight or nine – to the oldest and most illustrious, everyone respected him and accepted him. Jayne Munro, Inter-Gold Olympic aspirant, would swoop over to offer advice. Mrs Mottistone, who had already trained four British champions, greeted him warmly over coffee after berating him for hours upon the ice. He did not have to do or say anything. He was a skater. That was enough . . .

In the two years since he had started skating regularly, he had become used to mockery.

"Crispin!" Kass's voice twanged, "If we may have the pleasure of your company for a moment . . ."

"Er, yes, sir," Paul jumped.

"We were discussing quadratic equations, Crispin, but no doubt you have found something infinitely more interesting out on the drive, hmm? Or perhaps we were thinking about triple selkos or something, is that it? Well, I can always arrange for you to write down all your fascinating reflections after school this evening if you like . . . ?"

"No, sir," Paul said quickly, "Sorry, sir."

"Hmm. Well." Kass chuckled, "We would all be grateful, Crispin, if, in future, you would keep your thoughts about skating – on ice?"

"Yes, sir," Paul smiled obediently. "Ha. Ha."

Paul stuck his head through the door of the cricket pavilion. He peered quickly from right to left. There was no one on the drive. He drew back quickly and looked at his watch. A quarter to two. In just fifteen minutes, half the school would be up here to watch or to play in cricket matches. He whistled between his teeth and stamped impatiently on the bare boards. He couldn't afford to be seen here. Not like this.

So, soon as lunch was over, he had run out here to change. He wanted as much time as possible to practise at the rink. But if one of his schoolfellows saw the sparkling crimson suit and bow-tie which he wore beneath his overcoat, life would no longer be worth living at Springhill.

Outside, a car engine hummed and throbbed. Paul stepped eagerly forward. His mother's white Golf crept through the gates. He sighed his relief. He waited until the car stopped right opposite the pavilion, then glanced quickly over his shoulders, and ran.

"For heaven's sake," his mother grit her teeth and released the handbrake, "I cannot see the need for all this absurd cloak and dagger stuff."

"Well," Paul shrugged. He fastened his seat-belt. "You know."

"Just because you're afraid of a little teasing."

"It wouldn't just be a little teasing if they saw me looking like this," Paul sighed, "I'd never hear the last of it. No point in giving them more ammunition."

"Oh, the hell with them," June Crispin turned the car on the carriage sweep beneath the school. It kicked up a spurt of gravel. "Anyhow, I'm sorry I'm late. Your father kept me." Mr Crispin always became "Paul's father" when in bad odour, just as Paul became "his son" when he was in the doghouse. "Are you all set?"

"Yup. You remembered the skates?"

"I'm not stupid, you know. Of course I remembered the skates. Stop fussing. We'll be there in plenty of time."

"I need a good practice. We had gym this morning. My co-ordination's all over the place."

"Yes, well, you'll have plenty of time. Just lie back and have a snooze now. It's going to be a long day."

Paul nodded. He had become accustomed over the past few years to cat-napping whenever the opportunity arose. He rested his head on the window, pulled his overcoat close about him and slept almost at once.

"Anna!" Gabriella dragged her duster down the marble mantel and replaced the Chelsea figure.

"Yes!" Anna called from downstairs.

"You finished yet?"

"Nearly!"

"Bring up the furniture polish when you come, will you?"

"OK!"

"And a cup of tea!" Gabriella laughed and threw herself down into a deep, chintz-covered armchair.

"OK! I'll just be a second!"

Downstairs, Anna squeezed the last drops of dirty water from the mop and surveyed her work. The kitchen floor gleamed like virgin ice. The plates and glasses lay dried and polished on the work-surface.

Their employers had had a party the previous night. The dining-room, the kitchen – even the bedrooms and the bathroom – had been scattered with dirty glasses, ashtrays piled high with cigarette-ends and cherry-pips, and plates smeared with blood-red sauce.

Anna kicked off her shoes and tiptoed in stockinged feet to the kettle. While the water heated, she emptied the dirty water down the sink and shoved the bucket in the cupboard. She leaned back against the sink unit and exhaled noisily. For a moment she closed her eyes. Her shoulders slumped.

She was almost as tall as her mother now. What little could be seen of her hair beneath the blue and green headscarf was a bit lighter and wavier than Gabriella's. Her eyelashes were long and glossy. Her lips were full and slightly sullen in repose – lips quick to smile, to pout or to cry. Pale blue overalls covered everything else but slim, black-stockinged legs.

Clouds of steam from the kettle-spout barged one another up the sweating window-pane. Anna's eyes snapped open. They were clear and brown as the tea that she made. She put a spoonful of honey in her mother's mug and milk in both. She trotted up the spiral staircase. "Mama?"

"Hi," Gabriella reached out lazily, "I'm whacked."

"Me too. These people are pigs."

"Nope. Just humans. We'd probably do the same if we could have friends around and could afford someone to clean up afterwards."

"Well, humans are pigs then."

Anna strolled over to the window and pulled back the heavy velvet curtains. She looked down across Prince of Wales Drive to the bobbing trees in Battersea Park. "Is there much still to do?"

"No, just the tables."

"You stay still. I'll do them," Anna sighed.

"Oh, thank you, darling," Gabriella stretched luxuriously. "So what time does the competition start?"

"Seven o'clock, but I've got to practise a lot this afternoon."

"What do you have to do?"

"Same as before," she looked up from her polishing with a smile. "Only better."

"Well, you're doing pretty well. Four firsts and two seconds this year."

"Yup, but these are just club competitions. If I'm going to do well in the nationals, there's a lot more to do."

"And a lot of teaching," Gabriella sighed. "I know. If you and I worked every hour of the day, we still wouldn't be able to afford the amount of teaching you need."

"I know," Anna's voice shook as she rubbed the tabletop. "It's not your fault. Maybe one day I'll get a grant."

But she knew that there would be no grant. Grants were for those who had attained Inter-Gold and done well in national competitions. She had worked her way up to Inter-Silver thanks to hard work, kind teachers and Tracey Coombes, a pretty, rich, lazy blonde girl who passed on to Anna some of the lessons that she received. Gabriella had swallowed her pride too and asked her parents for help. They had paid for new skates and for some lessons, but the money had soon run out.

Skating had supplied Gabriella with a small but valuable source of extra income. The colourful costumes and the graceful movements of the skaters provided her with first-class subjects for photographs which she sold to the skaters themselves or to their parents. As her circle of acquaintances at the rink grew, rink-managers, too, commissioned her photographs for brochures, programmes and publicity. This extra money however was only enough to buy ice-time. Anna now needed intensive coaching if she was to make further progress. Coaching cost a lot more than they could afford.

Anna had proved talented on skates from the outset. Where to some the principal joy of skating lay in solitude and concentration, to Anna it lay in the freedom of movement, the poise with which she could speed across the ice. She felt elegant and much taller and somehow contrived to persuade the audience of the fact. Spectators frequently failed to recognize her when they met her after a performance, for, on ice, she was transformed. Her eyes sparkled. Her skin glowed. Her expression became confident and almost aloof. She was beautiful then.

"You going to win tonight, then?" asked Tracey.

"I don't know," Anna looked up from lacing her boots.

"Well, you'll beat all of us, that's for sure."

"Maybe, but we don't know who's coming from other clubs. Anyhow, you never know. I could make a mess of it. You might win."

"I doubt it," Tracey laughed. "I'm not the dedicated type. I like to do a little of everything. I mean, you never have time for anything else, do you?"

"No. I don't enjoy anything else as much as skating."

"Well, that's why you're good. Me now, I like skating and riding and eating and talking and dancing and – you know," she shrugged and smiled.

There was something about Tracey which made it needless for her to explain that "you know". She had thin blonde hair and glossy lips and large grey eyes far too innocent to be innocent. There was a gap between her front teeth through which her tongue-tip protruded. Her body was trim and tight, her movements almost arrogantly uninhibited. She stood now and raised one foot on to the low bench beneath the lockers. She finished tying her bootlaces, turned, stretched and grinned. "Come on, you can show me how you manage those toe-loops. They scare the hell out of me."

Gabriella crouched by the side of the rink. Her camera clicked and purred, clicked and purred. She was photographing Paul Crispin, though she did not know his name. She had chosen him as a subject simply because, of the four people on the ice, he was clearly the most proficient and had the best lines. He went into his jumps with verve, came out of them with poise.

She lowered the camera and straightened. Anna and Tracey stepped on to the rink, giggling. They waved. Gabriella waved back and walked up the ramp towards the glass-fronted cafeteria. She had a long wait ahead of her.

She bought a cup of tea and a Danish pastry and sat at a table overlooking the ice. Beneath, Anna and Tracey circled the rink. Tracey copied Anna. Several times she fell and laughed uproariously. The boy whom Gabriella had photographed seemed to pay no attention. He skated intently, practising spin after spin, jump after jump, edge after edge until he was satisfied.

"May I sit?" the voice from above her was soft and expressionless as distant muffled drums.

Gabriella looked up. The man above her was tall and very thin. He wore dark blue cords, a black polo-neck and a black leather jacket. A band of sand-coloured hair flopped over a face that might once almost have been called pretty, but there were lines now about his eyes and deep long lines from his nose to the corners of his mouth. His expression was doleful.

"Of course," Gabriella smiled faintly.

"Thank you," the man said politely. He slid in behind the table opposite her. He did not look at her or at the skaters but concentrated very hard on stirring his coffee.

His expression so closely resembled that of an abandoned dog that Gabriella felt that she must talk to him. "Have you got children competing here?" she asked.

"No."

"Oh, I have. My daughter. She is very good."

"Hm."

"That's her in the red and white."

He looked up briefly with pale blue eyes. They were very wet. He watched Anna briefly, said "Oh," and turned back to his coffee.

"She has got her Silver." Gabriella persisted, "We hope that she will go for the British Junior championships this year."

"She is not good enough," the man pronounced.

Gabriella had been about to bite her Danish pastry, but her hand stopped and her mouth stayed open. "What . . .?" she gaped. She took a deep breath. "No," she said, her vowels now very flat, "Not yet. She needs training, of course."

"Even then," the man shrugged, "I doubt that she is good enough."

"But . . . but . . ." Gabriella stammered, "but you are very rude! What do you mean, she is not good enough? What do you know about it?"

"I do not insult your daughter," the man shook his head wearily, "I tell the truth. I see a beautiful woman. I sit with her because I like beautiful women. My English is not very good and perhaps I am nervous a little, so I do not speak much. I see a girl who is a very good skater, but not a great athlete. I say so. It is all." He shrugged again, but this time he smiled.

It was a brilliant, infectious, childlike smile. Gabriella was hard put not to return it. Fellow-feeling for a stranger in a strange land made her bite back the tirade of abuse which was already fully formed in her mind. "Well, there is no problem," she said disdainfully, "because I cannot afford the training. But you are wrong."

"I have been wrong," the man said in his deadpan voice, "but very few times."

Gabriella's lips narrowed into a thin straight line. "Yes, well," she said. She slurped her coffee noisily and turned her whole body away from him. For the next twenty minutes, she pretended to think of nothing but the skaters.

Anna and Tracey had noticed Paul from the moment that they stepped on to the ice, but his ferocious frown of concentration had daunted them from attempting any introductions. Anna had noticed his technique as she and Tracey had warmed up. He was good, and above all, she noted, he was a perfectionist. Where she was too impatient to stop in the middle of a routine, too eager to enjoy the sensation of freedom and speed, he would check himself if so much as a single step was not to his liking, and would go back to start the whole figure again.

For all his single-mindedness, however, Paul had not failed to observe the two girls. Out of the corner of his eye, he watched them skating. Anna was clearly the better of the two, but Tracey – Tracey gave him a curious tickling sensation in his throat, and when first she sped past him, all soft bronzed skin and wet lips, he bungled a simple three-turn and had to practise it five times before he got it right. When she fell, stockinged legs splayed, he wanted to rush over and help her up. Instead, he scowled, and kept skating.

"He's nice," Tracey nodded towards him as she and Anna took a breather on the side of the rink.

Anna's lips twitched. "He's a good skater. Not exactly a charmer, though, is he?"

"Oh, I don't know," Tracey grinned and gulped air, "I quite like that. A mean man," she parodied herself, "knows where 'e's going and all that. Better than the sort that drool all over you."

"Yeah, well," Anna shrugged, "You're welcome to him. Maybe if you fall down right in front of him, he'll pick you up."

"Or the other way round," Tracey flicked her hair back from her brow, "Or maybe he'll kick me in the head. Great. Do you know who he is?"

"Nope," Anna smiled. "Don't know and don't care. Come on. Let's skate."

It was not Tracey who fell directly in front of Paul. It was Anna.

It might have been because she could hear his breathing and the swishing of his skates behind her. She was doing a little jazz routine of her own devising and standing almost still, when suddenly her left foot shot forward. Her arms described two rapid circles and she sat down hard.

Tracey whooped from the other end of the rink. "That's a good one!" she shouted, "Can you show me how to do it?"

Anna cocked a snook at her. "Come on," said a tetchy voice just above her. She looked up. The boy in the crimson suit was holding out his hand. He frowned irritably down at her. She took his hand and pulled herself to her feet. "Be careful," he said, "I could've hurt you." He turned and made to skate off again.

"Hold it!" Anna called at his back.

He turned, questioning.

"I suppose you never fell," she snapped. "I suppose you're too good to fall. You've got no manners, anyhow, that's for sure. *Sei un stronzo*!"

She moved off, head held high, right arm extended, a small smile on her lips. Paul watched her go, astonished.

Round pink spots appeared in his cheeks. A minute later, Anna had rejoined Tracey and he heard them talking quietly and laughing as they skated. The pink spots grew until his ears seemed to throb.

The absurd thing was that those few curt words that he had spoken had been intended as an introduction. They just had not come out right. He cursed himself for his ineptitude as he dragged himself from the rink, but, he told himself, even had he been downright rude, he would not have expected so violent and immediate a reaction from that weird foreign girl with the flashing eyes and the tumbling curls of brown hair.

Later that evening Anna shifted nervously from foot to foot and bit her lower lip. She was next on.

Her hair was piled high on her head now and neatly tied in a bun. She tugged nervously at the ringlet which hung down by her right ear. It was dark here in the competitors' entrance, and she could only see one third of the brilliantly lit rink. She could hear well enough though – the music, the sudden bursts of applause from the packed tiers of seats. Her closest rival, Tessa Sharp, was evidently doing well.

Occasionally she saw Tessa's smiling face, her sequin-encrusted pale blue costume, her bubbly blonde hair as she swung round at this end of the rink. Tessa came from Queen's. She was eighteen months younger than Anna but had the added advantage of looking at least three years her junior. Tessa looked cute.

Anna led her by just 0.4 of a point after the compulsory figures and the short programme. Tessa had messed up her landing on the double loop, but Anna had gone out of synch on the spin combination. The free programme carried fifty per cent of the total score. If Tessa made no blunders – if Anna heard no groans from the audience in the next two minutes – there would still be everything to do.

There were no groans. As the music tinkled to a close, the audience roared and stamped and cheered. The marks were read out over the tannoy.

Technical merit:

Artistic impression:

Tessa simpered sweetly as she passed Anna. She knew that she would be hard to beat.

Anna pushed out into the centre of the ice. The crowd applauded. The lights span around, dazzling her.

"And now," the tinny tannoy crackled, "a local girl, lying first after the compulsory figures and the short programme, Anna – Lombardi!"

Anna stood stock still, her right arm crooked beneath her chin, her left extended behind her. Her weight rested on her left leg. A breeze from somewhere ruffled her hair. A clarinet and an oboe wailed. She did not move. Then strings started up in bouncy unison. The bent arm slowly straightened, the left leg bent. Without a perceptible movement to impel her, she was sliding slowly forward.

She had chosen three numbers from *West Side Story*: *Something's Coming* was breezy, brisk and smooth; *America* vigorous, syncopated and jazzy; *Tonight* romantic, heroic and slow. Each in its way gave Anna the chance to do what she did best – to dance, to act, to show off her natural elegance and sense of drama. She had never felt happy striking whimsical poses – flapping limp hands, sticking her bottom out, wagging imaginary tails, wagging fingers and pouting – all the Olga Korbutt-style tricks favoured by so many female skaters. She could not see, to start off with, what they had to do with skating, nor did they display the poise and the emotional force which she could bring to her performances.

Something's Coming went beautifully. The spin combination which had cost her so many hours of effort felt perfectly centred and absolutely right. The double loop/double axel jump combination was as easy and natural as in her dreams.

She threw herself with enormous verve into *America*, snarling and preening and strutting like some Latin ancestor ten years her senior. The audience clapped in time with the music.

Anna did not have to think now about what she was doing. The music, the speed, the sound of the audience, all served to numb conscious thought. She acted on reflex learned in months of practice. Just as a bird surely does not need to think about flying so soon as it is on the wing, so did it seem natural to Anna to jump, to turn, to spin in time with the music.

If in *America* she had seemed older and more sophisticated, in *Tonight*, she became the young "star-crossed" lover, Maria or Juliet, eagerly looking forward to her meeting with her lover yet aware of impending sorrow. She nearly fell on landing after an adventurous jump, but she seemed scornfully to kick away the error as though it were something clinging at her foot, preventing her from keeping her appointment.

Technical merit was a long way from most people's thoughts – which was an eloquent tribute to the technical merit of her performance – when at the end she knelt, grieving, in a single spotlight at the centre of the rink. The music ended. There was a moment's pause before the applause came. That moment's pause told Anna that she had won.

The applause crashed over her in great waves, shaking

the walls of the rink. She stood, blinking, and curtseyed low. She looked like someone rudely awakened from a dream.

"Well," she said blithely, as she skated off the rink into Gabriella's arms, "that was all right."

Gabriella smiled and sniffed. "Yes," she nodded, "it was OK. Actually," she whispered, "it was quite good, really." Suddenly she laughed. "Oh, *dio*, my daughter is more English than the English! It was great. Really really great."

Anna sighed. "It felt good, but, oh," she stamped, "it could be so much better."

"I know, darling," Gabriella looked up at the lights above her daughter's head. "I know."

"Paul, come quickly," his mother shook his shoulder. "There's someone you've got to meet."

"Hold on," Paul shook his head irritably. "This girl, the girl on the ice this afternoon . . ." he nodded down at the rink where Anna neared the end of her programme. "She's not bad."

"Yes, but I can't keep him waiting, Paul. You've got to come *now*."

"Sh!" Paul commanded and leaned forward, his forearms on his knees, "Just a minute."

"Paul, it's *important*. Now!"

He turned round, undisguised irritation on his face, "What is it?"

"Just come with me and you'll see. Quickly!"

Paul sighed and stood just as Anna finished her programme. He was applauding as he sidestepped past the other performers and followed his mother up the aisle and down the dark corridor to the cafeteria.

A tall fair man in a black leather jacket stood intently

watching the skating below. "Er, Mr Bunin," Mrs Crispin's voice had an appeasing smile in it.

"Sh." The tall man did not move.

"Oh. Yes." Mrs Crispin said nervously. She stood by his side and gestured to Paul to do the same. Together they watched a girl in green, red and yellow slithering ineptly about the ice. Her tracings were palsied, her movements inelegant. Her jumps were timorous hops which nonetheless resulted almost invariably in her sprawling on the ice. One minute into her programme, Bunin shook his head and turned away with a groan.

"Yes?" he raised his eyebrows, "What was it, Mrs . . .?"

"Crispin. June Crispin," she beamed. "I was telling you about my son, Mr Bunin. Well, this is Paul. Paul," she gulped, "this is Grigor Bunin."

She announced the name as though she were telling a risqué joke. Obviously it was meant to mean something to Paul. It didn't. He thought that perhaps he had heard it somewhere before, but he could not think where. He smiled politely and shook Bunin's hand. The tall man's weary eyes crinkled into a smile. "You skate?" he said.

"Yes." Paul nodded, "I'm only Silver, though . . ."

"He was second in the compulsory figures this evening," Mrs Crispin urged, "and the person who beat him was two years older than him, and he was fourth in the short programme but he'd have won if it hadn't been for an accident . . ."

"He should not have accidents," Bunin proclaimed.

"No, well, of course, with a bit more training . . . I mean, accidents do happen to everyone, don't they? Particularly when you're Paul's age. But you must watch his free programme, Mr Bunin. It's quite brilliant. Mrs Mottistone – well, you know Mrs Mottistone, from

Richmond, of course – well, she worked it out. It's won at several contests like this, and then we're going for the National Junior . . ."

"I will watch," Bunin said grimly, and turned back to the rink.

"Thank you so much, Mr Bunin," Mrs Crispin gushed at his back, "Thank you. Come along now, Paul, we'd better leave Mr Bunin to watch . . ."

Paul shrugged and followed her. She had passed through the door when he heard Bunin's voice behind him. "Paul?"

Paul turned. "Yes, sir?"

"Good luck."

Paul's face relaxed into a grin. "Thanks, Mr Bunin."

Bunin turned back to the skating. Paul closed the door quietly behind him. His mother was waiting for him in the corridor. "Isn't it wonderful? Grigor Bunin, here!"

"Who's Grigor Bunin?" Paul asked innocently.

"Grigor Bunin? You know who Grigor Bunin is. Don't be silly. You're just being obtuse, Paul. You know perfectly well. Bunin! Bunin and Petrovich! The dancers! World champions forever in the 'sixties, Olympic gold medallists. Bunin was training the Russian team when he defected. *You* remember. It was just four or five years ago!"

"Mum, that was when I was ten or eleven, and, as for the 'sixties, I wasn't even born then!"

"Oh. No. Nor you were. Well, anyhow, he's a great ice dancer, and we talked earlier, and – well, he's going to watch your programme. That's good, isn't it?"

"I dunno. Why?"

"Well – it – it always helps to have contacts, doesn't it? Of course it does. He could be very useful, one day. You never know."

"No, Mum," Paul smiled to himself in the darkness. "You never know."

"Let's go and celebrate," Gabriella greeted Anna as she came from the changing-room. "There's a little *trattoria* owned by a friend of Lorenza's cousin from Bologna. We could have a bowl of pasta or something."

"Not now, Mama," Anna ran her fingers through her newly released hair. "I'd like to watch the men."

"OK," Gabriella had expected it, "but we'll have to leave by ten if we're going to eat and get you to bed. I'll take some pictures. You go up and watch. I'll pick you up when it's time to leave."

Anna nodded and smiled. She looked very different now from the girl in overalls this morning, very different, too, from the skater earlier in the evening. She wore a loose white tee-shirt and tight-fitting designer jeans – a present from her grandfather. She walked with a loose-limbed, slouching gait. Some trace of the arrogance so manifest in her skating remained perhaps in the careless manner in which she flung her coat over her right shoulder and barged through the double swing-doors.

She slid into a seat next to Tracey who, still in her costume, leaned back, her knee raised on the seat in front of her.

"Well done, kid," Tracey whispered. "You looked really great out there."

"Thanks. You were pretty good too. Fourth, wasn't it?"

"Yeah," Tracey chewed noisily on her gum. "Not bad, but when I look at you, I think I ought to take up hang-gliding or jumping off high buildings or something."

"I promise I'll come and watch," Anna giggled.

"Thanks a ton, superspag."

"What are these men like?"

"Lousy. Your friend from this afternoon has just been on. He was the best so far. Technically perfect and good lines, but still hard-faced and unfeeling. Think, think, think all the time. No – no – sparkle, you know? No charm."

"Still fancy him then?"

"Yup. Well, he's different, anyhow. Weird, but interesting."

Anna laughed, then, "Don't think much of this wimp, I must say."

"Nah, well. They can't help it. It's just the natural superiority of the female of the species. Any one of us could beat him. Most of these guys, in fact."

"I know. There's not so much competition for the boys, and it's usually the ones with bodies like prawns who take it up. If they're natural athletes they go in for football or boxing or something."

"More fool them. What about our friend Paul Crispin, then? Wonder why he became a skater?"

"Too goddamned rude to get on with anyone else, I should think."

"You've really got it in for him, haven't you?"

"Well," Anna turned up her nose and dismissed Paul with a flap of the hand. "He's a pain, that's all."

"Mr Bunin! Mr Bunin!" June Crispin stage whispered as she gave chase along the front tier of seats.

"Excuse me," Bunin bent, "excuse me . . ."

"Oh, sorry," Mrs Crispin followed, "Sorry, excuse me. Oh. I am so sorry. Mr *Bunin*!"

"Yes?" said Bunin languidly as he sank into a chair.

"What did you think of Paul, Mr Bunin?" she clambered over him to a chair of her own.

"Not good." Bunin sighed. His eyes followed the skater on the rink.

"Not good?" Mrs Crispin almost shrieked. "What do you mean, not good?"

Bunin folded his arms and raised his eyebrows as though astonished that she should ask such a question. "Not good," he explained.

"In – in what way, not good?"

"Too old. No personality. Not his fault. Still. He works hard, however. He is serious. That is good. He will never be a champion. Pity."

"But Mrs Mottistone says . . ."

"Mrs Mottistone talks about minor amateur contests. Yes, I am sure that he could win those and get a job teaching at a rink like this. That is what you want?"

"No," Mrs Crispin said with heartfelt emotion. "But we're prepared to pay for the very best trainers, anything . . ."

"Money will not make him two years younger, Mrs . . . No. He will never be a champion."

"But, Mr Bunin . . ." June Crispin implored.

"Please, Mrs . . . I am trying to watch the others. You will please bring your son here at nine o'clock on Monday morning. I will have something to say to him. Thank you."

"But he has to go to school . . ."

"You will have to work that out. Excuse me, please, Mrs . . ." Bunin sighed deeply and unfolded his lean frame. With a casual nod to Mrs Crispin, he turned and trotted up the aisle. With a deep sigh, he threw himself down just one seat away from Anna and Tracey.

Gabriella ignored him when she came up and saw him

there. She covered the telephoto lens of her camera and beckoned to Anna from the aisle. Anna placed her hand on Tracey's wrist for a moment. They exchanged good-byes. Anna arose.

Bunin got up and stepped out into the aisle to let her pass. "Madam," he said softly to Gabriella, "I have something to say to you."

"Yes?" Gabriella answered shortly.

"Come with me. The music is too loud."

"I don't think I have much to say to you," said Gabriella but she followed him to the doors. He pushed them and held them open as Gabriella and Anna walked out into the foyer. Every word here resounded as in a public swimming-pool. The music seemed distant.

"I," said Bunin, "am Grigor Bunin." He paused to allow his words to take effect.

Their effect was not dramatic. Gabriella frowned as though trying to remember. Anna nodded and smiled. "I thought I recognized you," she said. She held out her hand. "I have seen you in photographs."

"Good," Bunin inclined his head and took her hand. "I think maybe I can help you. Be here please at nine o'clock on Monday morning."

"OK," Anna spoke quietly and immediately.

"One moment, please," Gabriella stepped forward. "My daughter has school, and she's not going to miss classes just to hear you telling her she's no good."

Bunin gave his usual expressive shrug. "As you wish, madam. I do not see that she can become good unless she is told where she is no good. It is up to you. You come or not. I will be here at nine o'clock on Monday. If you are not here by five past, I will be gone. I have little time to waste."

"We'll be there," said Anna. She squeezed her mother's hand hard. "Thank you Mr Bunin."

Bunin nodded once, zipped up his leather jacket and strode with the springy steps of the athlete to the main doors and out into the night.

"I can't think what that man can have to say," Mrs Crispin announced over breakfast the following morning. "All he could say was 'no good', 'he will not be a champion', 'he is too old.' Hardly a constructive approach. I'd have thought."

"'Bout time someone talked some sense," Paul's father mumbled through marmalade. "I mean, who cares whether Paul is any good at cavorting around on ice, hmm? He's got a normal life to live like anyone of us. What's going to happen when he leaves school, hmm? Qualifications; several cupro-nickel medals for ice-skating. Fat lot of good that'll do him. It's about time you started thinking about that, June."

"I agree," Katie picked at her grapefruit. "I always said he'd be no good anyhow. It's so shaming, really. 'What does your brother do?' 'Oh, he's in the army', 'Oh, he's up at Oxford', 'Oh, he just got five 'A' levels'. 'And you, Katie? What does your brother do?' 'Oh, he plays the sugar-plum fairy on ice.' I mean, *really*."

"What gets me about skating, seriously," Mr Crispin at last turned to Paul who was unconcernedly tucking in to eggs and bacon, "is – well, I mean, I can imagine, I could understand if it was something *useful*. You know, boxing is to do with survival. It hones your skills. Fencing. Rugby, for example. Teaches you to think fast. Deal with your fellow man. But skating? Useful for a Norwegian when he needs to get a doctor, I suppose, but not much use really to your average English businessman, eh?"

Paul sighed. "No, Dad. I know."

"Oh, we can't expect you to understand anything about the arts, of course," June Crispin's lips tightened. She swung from her chair and laid her empty plate down with a clatter on the side. "I suppose you've never heard of art for art's sake?"

"Yes, actually, I have. Always struck me as a daft idea, and anyhow, I'm damned if I'm going to see Paul's future compromised for the sake of two or three years' showing off. Sorry, Paul. Look, let's make an agreement. If this Bunin chap says there's no future in it, you'll give it up, just treat it as a hobby from now on, okay? If he says you can make something of it, well, all right. I'll button my lip so long as your schoolwork doesn't suffer and I'll continue to foot the bills. You must see that there's no point in forking out all this money and spending all this time if it can't come to anything, hmm?"

Paul poured himself a cup of coffee and looked around the table. His father smiled indulgently. Katie grinned with undisguised malice and sipped herb tea. His mother stood by the toaster. She shrugged.

"Well, Paul?" his father urged, "We'll let this Russky decide. Deal?"

Paul's breakfast felt very heavy. Something whimpered in his stomach. His shoulders slumped. "All right," he said quietly. "It's a deal."

It was a good sort of day for a Monday, the sort of day when you actually feel glad to arrive at the warmth and light of the office, shop or classroom and complain with your workmates about conditions outside. The sky was grey. The streets were grey. The pavements were wet and crackled like tinfoil beneath Anna's feet as she and Gabriella walked from the tube station to the rink. The air felt like somebody else's bath grown cold. They walked briskly, scarves wrapped tight around their necks and mouths. They did not talk.

There were no lights on in the foyer. They tried the glass doors but found them locked. Gabriella hammered on the door. "Wouldn't surprise me if he wasn't even here," she grumbled. "Probably does this all the time. Probably a drunk." She beat at the door with a clenched fist. "Come on . . ." she murmured and shifted from foot to foot, "Come *on*!"

"Calm down," Anna reproved. "We've only been here two seconds. He'll be here soon."

"If he's here at all."

"*Eccolo*!" Anna nodded to where a door opened inside and a guillotine blade of light sliced across the vinyl floor. Bunin's silhouetted figure in the doorway was unmistakable.

"Good morning, signora Lombardi," he bowed low over Gabriella's hand and flashed a quick, impudent smile at her, then straightened, suddenly stern again.

"Good morning, Mister Bunin."

"Good morning, Anna. Come on in."

Both women shivered as they stepped into the warm blast of air from above the door. Bunin's footfalls echoed as he led them towards the light. "Come on in," he repeated and stood back to allow them into the office.

Anna walked in. She stopped so suddenly that her mother bumped into her, pushing her two steps forward. Three paper cups steamed on the desktop. Behind one sat a middle-aged woman with fine features and greying auburn hair. Behind another, though only the top of his head showed above the desk, sat Paul Crispin.

He stood. "Um . . ." he said. "Hello." He glanced quickly up at Anna, then down at the desktop, then, querying, at Bunin.

Anna frowned and looked anywhere but at Paul.

"Right." Bunin squeezed into the tiny room and shut the door. "I think there are enough chairs. Sit, please."

There was a lot of shuffling and banging then as Gabriella and Anna sat opposite Paul and his mother. Bunin perched on the corner of the desk.

"Tea? Coffee?" he asked.

"No, thank you," said Anna evenly.

"Right. OK. Listen. I am Grigor Bunin. I am a skater. I saw both you children skating on Saturday. You, Anna, are good. You have great natural . . ." he flapped his fingers as he sought the right word, ". . . you are a good actor. You have – presence. You love skating. That is good. If you persist, if you train hard, if you are lucky, if you have money, you may have a reasonable career. Perhaps even British Champion. Probably not. Probably second, third to someone with more luck, more money. You have no money. You therefore have no chance.

"You," he turned to Paul, "are not so good. You work hard, you are strong, you are stubborn. That is good. You have no charisma, however. You will not win the hearts of the judges. You are a good technician. You may win some competitions because you fight, but nothing top class."

Paul's eyes grew hot as Bunin spoke. That was it. He clasped and unclasped his fingers. He looked at the floor, then up at the light. He blinked. He did not want to have to say anything. He did not trust his voice.

"And why should we believe your prophesies, Mr Bunin?" June Crispin demanded with a snap of her handbag clasp. Gabriella nodded agreement.

"Because I am Grigor Bunin," Bunin answered, surprised, "and perhaps I know more about these things than most people."

"You bring us here to tell us this?" Gabriella stood, her fists clenched. "You make our children miss school to listen to you destroying their confidence? We have work to do. We have no interest in your opinions, thank you very much . . ."

"In that case," Bunin stood and faced her, "you are stupid. Criticism is worth more than flattery. Your children could waste years of their lives striving for an excellence that they cannot attain. You, madam, could spend thousands of pounds which you have not got. But I have asked you here to make to you a proposition, so please – sit – down."

They glared at one another for a moment, then Gabriella tossed her head, mumbled something and sat.

Paul leaned forward and blinked at the bottom drawer of the desk. His bowed head was now barely visible. His mother's hand reached out and held his for a moment, but he pulled away. Anna slumped like a stringless puppet and stared straight ahead of her.

"My proposition," Bunin resumed, "is simple and will benefit both of you – all of you. These two children are amongst the most promising that I have seen since I came to England. They both have qualities which are necessary. They will dance together. I will train them."

He picked up his paper cup, made to drink from it, saw that it was empty and crumpled it in his fist. He flung it into the tin waste-paper bin by Paul's feet. There was silence.

Paul took a deep breath and sat up. He looked at Anna. A small nervous smile touched his lips.

Anna turned away to look at Bunin. "No," she said.

"It might be a good idea," Gabriella said softly.

"No."

"And why not, may I ask?" June Crispin demanded. "I can see some sense in Mr Bunin's suggestion."

"No."

"But why not, in God's name?"

"Because I do not like him." She was sullen.

"You don't even know him, girl."

"I know him enough. I do not want to dance with him."

"Paul?" Bunin asked.

"Well . . . I mean, I've never danced. I don't know. If she's against it, I suppose that's all there is to it."

"Oh, she's just being hysterical," Mrs Crispin added as she swept back her hair with one rapid aggressive movement of her hand. "If Mr Bunin says that they have a better chance . . ."

"I say that it is their only chance, madam," Bunin broke in. "I will train Miss Lombardi free of charge. If she refuses – well, that will be the end of her skating career anyhow."

Anna turned to Gabriella with tears in her eyes. Gabriella nodded, "I'm afraid it's true. You know it is."

"And as for the fact that you dislike this poor young man," Bunin laughed, "nothing could be better. There will be times over the next few months when you will hate him and he will hate you. I am suggesting that you work together, not that you fall in love. Which is more important to you, Anna? Your love of skating or your dislike of Paul?"

Anna glared at Paul. "Skating." She spoke like an automaton.

"Good. Good! And you, Paul?"

"I'd like to try."

"Excellent. You will not regret it."

"You say you will train this girl free of charge," Mrs

Crispin indicated Anna with disdain. "What about my son?"

"Madam," Bunin's eyes rolled heavenward, "A few days ago, you said to me, 'We are prepared to pay for the very best trainers', is that not so?"

"Yes," Mrs Crispin said cautiously, "but . . ."

"Well, I am the very best trainer. I too have to live, you know. I am prepared to train Miss Lombardi free because her delightful mother has no money. You have lots of money. You pay. Besides," he said smoothly and swivelled round to eye Gabriella, "Signora Lombardi and I are friends."

Gabriella opened her mouth. For once, no words came.

"So," Bunin smiled, "is it agreed?"

He looked at them one by one. No one answered. "Paul," Bunin frowned, "Is it agreed?"

"Yes," Paul croaked. "Thank you, Mr Bunin."

"Anna?"

"Yes." She flashed a quick glance at Paul then looked demurely down at her hands in her lap, "All right."

"I think you are forgetting something?" Bunin prompted.

Anna pouted. "Thank you," she said quietly.

"And you, Mrs Crispin?"

"Well," June Crispin shrugged, "I suppose it's all right, if you're sure it's the best thing."

"I am certain."

"Though of course we'll have to discuss the money side of things."

"Of course," Bunin bowed, "and finally, you, Signora Lombardi?"

He raised an eyebrow and looked into Gabriella's eyes. A reluctant smile twisted her lips. "All right," she said.

"You seem to have all the answers, Mr Bunin. It is a good idea. Thank you."

"Good." Bunin gave her one of his extra dazzling smiles. "Right. We are wasting skating time."

"One, two, three, and . . . no, no, no! The edges have to flow into one another. Try it again."

Paul sighed deeply. Anna glowered at Bunin. They returned to the edge of the rink. Paul stiffly put his right arm around the back of Anna's waist. She extended her left arm so that the hand rested on his.

"Right." Bunin commanded from the centre of the ice. "Make those three-turns *smooth*. OK, one, two, three, turn, better! And, one two . . . What's the matter with you?" he skated smoothly over to them.

"Well, look," Paul grabbed both Anna's hands and tugged them about as though she were a doll. "When we do this . . ." she span resignedly in his arms, "and come out of the turn, she's leaning on me, so I can't get on to the outside edge."

"Oh, so it's my fault," Anna pulled away from Paul.

"Well, yes, it is."

"Of course," she slapped away his right hand, "It couldn't be Mr high and mighty Crispin's fault, could it?"

"That is enough, Anna," Bunin sighed. "For the hundredth time, if you want to indulge in high drama, go and be an actress. We are concentrating on ice-skating. There is no room for temperament here. Paul is right. You must not lean. Is there a problem with the arm movements there?"

And so it went on, hour after hour, day after day, the precise dissection of every step, every slightest movement in the American Waltz, the Blues, the Pasa Doble. Throughout the long summer holidays, the practice sessions started at seven o'clock in the morning and went on for five hours until the rink was opened to the public.

Bunin was often there for an hour or two, sometimes on the ice, sometimes just watching from the side, the inevitable paper cup of coffee steaming in his hand. The actual lessons took place at five o'clock every evening. Both Anna and Paul went to bed every evening at nine o'clock.

Curiously, neither of them felt tired. The constant succession of new challenges was frustrating but invigorating. Every difficulty could be overcome, and, on the rare occasions when everything worked perfectly, when both of them moved as one, all the hard work, all the squabbles, all the muscular aches and bruises seemed worthwhile.

The relationship between the two skaters could hardly be described as close. They met in the morning, exchanged brief greetings, and skated. Thereafter, not a word was spoken save about technical matters. Even when they stopped for a cup of coffee, the discussions concerned lifts, spins and steps.

Anna and Paul were constantly coming up with new ideas to embellish the formal dances. Some of these ideas were comic, but no one would have known it from the serious way in which they were put forward, discussed, practised and developed.

Occasionally, Paul ventured to make a joke; occasionally he asked Anna how she was or gently mocked her volatile temper, but they had nothing else to discuss. There were no tales of discos to tell, no accounts of new acquaintances or of adventures. The only dancing that they did was at the ice rink. They met no one but other skaters. Their only adventures occurred in the fantasy world of their dances. They skated, slept, skated, slept, and what spare time they had they spent in designing costumes or working out new routines. And curiously, although there were constant recriminations, some sort of mutual dependence grew up between them. They shared their triumphs and disasters, their ambitions and their disappointments. They worked to the same timetable, fought the same battles. Had you asked Anna if she liked Paul at the time, she would have looked puzzled at the question, then shrugged and admitted, "He's all right."

Paul, asked the same question of her, would have responded in the same way. He did not think of her as a girl in the same way, for example, as he thought of Tracey. Anna was his skating partner, that was all. He quite liked her, though he found her sudden changes of mood confusing.

Once, in early September, she was singing as she arrived with Gabriella at the rink. During their practice, she fell twice and parodied herself by impersonating a drunk, staggering all over the ice. Paul laughed, but eventually glanced at his watch and said, "Come on, Anna. We've got to work out this Starlight."

She ignored him and continued to clown to her mother.

"Anna," Paul pleaded, "come on. We can't waste time."

She turned her head and sneered, then resumed her gabbling and giggling to her mother.

"Anna," Paul spoke sharply through gritted teeth, "I don't want to waste any more time. Come *on*!"

"Shut up!" she snapped. She turned, and her face was pink with fury. "Who are you to give me orders? You're a bore. I'm sick of you! 'Come on, Anna.' 'We're wasting time, Anna.' Yes, sir, no, sir. Boring, boring, boring!"

Yet only two days later, Paul was sitting with Tracey in the cafeteria when Anna strode up to their table. "Come on, Paul," she said on a monotone, "I'm not here just to stand around while you enjoy yourself."

"Hold on," Paul laughed, startled. "We've only just got our coffee. It's hot!"

"Yeah, keep cool, will you, Annie?" Tracey soothed. "I'm not going to steal your partner away, you know. Just give us a moment to relax, will you?"

Anna looked from Paul to Tracey then back to Paul again. "OK," she breathed, "OK, but I'm not wasting my time. See you when you feel like doing some work, Paul."

She strutted off, and a moment later Paul saw her emerge on the ice. She skated straight over to Osbert Keevil, a slight, sallow boy of sixteen with oily black curly hair who never wore anything but black. Paul disliked Osbert. He disliked his ready, insincere smile, his soft voice, his unctuous manner, the clicking consonants and the flat vowels with which he spoke. Anna stood very close to him as she talked. Osbert smiled and bowed low with a flamboyant wave of the hand, then put his arm around her waist and led her in a smooth but unadorned Viennese Waltz.

"Oh, don't worry," Tracey laid a hand on Paul's knee, which made him gulp. "These Italians are temperamental, you know."

Five minutes later, Paul tapped Osbert's shoulder. Osbert turned and looked up at him with his usual smile. "Yes?"

Paul just stood over him and said nothing.

"Oh, I suppose you'll be wanting to practise with Anna. We have been enjoying ourselves, haven't we, Anna?"

"Yes. Thank you, Osbert," Anna smiled. "I'm afraid I have to get back to business now." She cast a withering glance at Paul as she stressed the word "business".

One thing Paul had learned about Anna. She never

apologized and she never bore a grudge. Five minutes after she had been yelling at him and swearing that she never wished to see him again, she would be happily skating and making plans as though nothing had happened.

Things became tougher when school started again. The timetable did not allow that Paul should make the daily trip up to Streatham, then back to school for nine o'clock, then back to Streatham in the evening. Amongst other things, the travelling proved more exhausting than the skating. His temper grew shorter. Bags appeared under his eyes. At times, towards the end of the evening sessions, his eyes would wander vaguely about the rink, his attention would stray and he would mumble nonsense.

At breakfast one cold morning Tony Crispin breezed in, brisk and crisp as ever. "Good morning, darling," he sang. He snapped off the lights. "Don't need those," he mumbled. He sat and unfolded a napkin. "Now!" he said for no particular reason. He began to open his mail. He read the letters quickly and sorted them into three small piles: circulars, bills and letters for personal attention. It was a practised routine. Read, pour coffee, read, sip, sigh, read, reach for toast, spread butter and marmalade while reading, munch, read . . .

"Oh, no," his voice made Mrs Crispin jump. "Oh no, no, no. This is just too much. No."

Mrs Crispin looked up from cutting Katie's grapefruit segments. "What is it, darling?" Her voice was full of apprehension, her expression of resignation.

"I have here," Mr Crispin waved the sheet of paper. "I have here a letter concerning a certain young man who as I recall, was once a member of this household. Doesn't seem to live here now, of course, but there. It is a letter of complaint. From his headmaster. I would be grateful, since you have been a major influence in this matter, if you would listen . . ." He smoothly pulled glasses, which had been unnecessary before, from his breast pocket and placed them portentously on his nose. He cleared his throat. "Dear Mr Crispin . . ."

"Hello, Daddy! Morning, Mummy!" Katie swept in. She wore a dressing-gown. The towel around her head steamed. "I'm doing a henna thing," she explained as she sat. "I've got to keep this thing on my head for twenty minutes and then when I take it off, my hair will be lustrous deep auburn."

"Katie . . ." her mother said warningly, "Sh."

Tony Crispin cleared his throat again. "Thank you," he said to an imaginary audience, "'Dear Mr Crispin, I share, as you know, your concern regarding the effect of Paul's extra-mural sporting activities upon his school-work. Hitherto, I have been pleasantly surprised by his progress. He has not always seemed to devote enough effort to his academic work, particularly in mathematics, but he has nonetheless retained his place in class and the projections for his GCSEs have been satisfactory.

"I would have continued to tolerate this somewhat unsatisfactory state of affairs, however, had it not been for a series of reports which have reached me over the past few weeks. Paul has consistently arrived late at school, sometimes missing as much as half an hour of his first class and, on two occasions, missing it altogether. It has further been reported to me that he is frequently incapable of paying the least attention and has now four times been found to be *sleeping in class*!'" Mr Crispin underlined these words with a shriek. He looked up at his wife, afforded her an accusing glare, shuddered and turned back to the letter. "'You will appreciate'," he read, "'that this situation cannot be allowed to continue.

I cannot blame Paul, as it is clear that his skating is placing an intolerable strain on him. I must therefore ask that he henceforth restrict his indulgence in this hobby to the weekend, at least until his GCSEs studies are completed. I would in any case prefer that he should become a full, participating member of the school. Experience has shown that excessive concentration on the development of one talent at the expense of others can only be deleterious.

"I look forward to hearing from you etcetera, etcetera,'" Mr Crispin laid down the letter with an air of infinite sorrow. There was silence for a while. Mrs Crispin bit her lip. Katie chewed on her grapefruit. "Well?" Mr Crispin said at last.

"Well what?"

"Well, you heard what he said, didn't you? Paul is *sleeping* in class, for God's sake! He's turning up late. His schoolwork is suffering. He's headed for the scrapheap, all because of this precious dancing business. You can't deny it now, June. It's gone too far. It's got to stop. I am going to ring Mr Moore and tell him that Paul is to return straight home this evening. No more of this gallivanting. I've had enough." He thumped the table with a clenched fist and stood. "I'll tell Paul this evening. I'll expect him to be here when I return."

"Good," Katie licked her lips. "I'm fed up with all this attention and money, all this Paul, Paul, Paul stuff. Just because he can go round and round on ice like a pneumatic drill or something. He's been getting too cocky. Do him good."

"I'll be back at six thirty, June," Mr Crispin said crisply. "I'll see you then, and we'll deal with this matter once and for all. All right? Good. Goodbye." He turned with a click of his shiny shoes and marched from the room.

Mrs Crispin ran for the telephone. "Hello," she said suddenly, "Hello, Streatham Ice Rink? Can I speak to Mr Bunin, please? Grigor Bunin."

"Right," was Mr Crispin's first word as he entered the hall that evening. It was wasted. There was no one to hear it. He took off his dripping overcoat and hung it on a hook. "Right," he repeated and pushed open the drawing-room door.

Paul sat on an armchair by the fire. A dark girl whom he did not recognize sat curled on the rug. She stood as he entered. On the sofa, Mrs Crispin was talking eagerly to a tall man with very long legs. His angular features cast deep shadows in the fluttering firelight. He too stood. He stepped forward. "Mr Crispin," his voice throbbed like the heart of the fire, "Grigor Bunin."

"Er – hello."

"And this," Bunin waved his long right hand, "is Anna Lombardi, Paul's partner. There was no means whereby I could tell her not to come to practice tonight, so I had to bring her with me."

"Oh," Mr Crispin frowned, "Yes, um. Fine. Good. No problem. Delighted to meet you, er . . . Anna." He shook her hand and looked irritably towards his wife and Paul. "Jolly good," he said and puffed a lot of air through his nose. "Right. Drink for anyone?"

"Lovely, darling," Mrs Crispin drawled. "A dry martini."

"And for you, Mr Bunin? Anna?"

"Thank you," said Anna, "Lemonade, please, or orange juice."

"And whisky for me, please, Mr Crispin."

"Certainly. Yes. Right." Tony Crispin tried to regain his composure as he busied himself with ice-cubes and bottles. "So!" he said cheerfully as he crossed the room with the drinks. "Yes. Good to see you. Now, you've probably heard, Mr Bunin, that we have a problem with Paul."

"Yes." Bunin nodded his thanks as he took the glass. "We have the same problem. His schoolwork is making skating very difficult."

"Er – yes." Mr Crispin sank into his own armchair, "But of course we don't see it quite like that. School must be our first priority. It is going to affect the whole of Paul's life. If it's a choice between school and skating, it's skating that will have to go."

"You talk about life after school," Bunin said, "and of course I agree with you that school is important, but do you realize that in a few months, when Anna and Paul take their Inter-Gold, they will already be qualified for a job which can give them an income for the rest of their lives?"

"As what?"

"As skating instructors."

"Yes, well, perhaps," Mr Crispin mused, embarrassed. "But it's not quite the sort of thing – well, we had hoped for something better for Paul."

"Tony!" Mrs Crispin chided.

Bunin held up a hand to silence protests. "I agree with you, Mr Crispin. I too would not want Paul – or Anna – just to be teachers. I think – I will not promise it – I think that they could be champions. British champions almost certainly, European champions perhaps, Olympic, world champions – who knows? Anything is possible. Serious champions, you know, make very, very large sums of money when they turn professional."

"Yes, yes, of course. Yes, I understand that, but it's all terribly speculative, isn't it? No, I'm afraid we've made our minds up here. There's nothing we can do about it. I'd like you to continue, of course," he turned to Paul, "but now, what with GCSEs, well, you've had a good innings, and you'll always be able to go back to it and enjoy it when you're older. Wonderful hobby, I'm sure. I'm sorry, but that's it."

"I disagree," said Mrs Crispin. She knocked her drink back in one. The wind groaned in the chimney. "I think that Paul can continue to skate and must continue to skate. It's not just him that will be affected here. It's young Anna too. They've both invested a great deal of time and effort into a partnership. It's totally unethical to propose dissolving that partnership merely because of unforeseen circumstances."

"Yes, well, maybe," Tony Crispin made a slicing gesture with his hand, "and I'm very sorry, Anna, but there's nothing I can do about it. Qualifications matter more than skating. That's it." He got up and took his wife's glass and his own over to the drinks trolley.

"That is not it," Mrs Crispin tried but failed to stem the acid that had crept into her tone. "I have a say in this matter and so has Paul. There are other schools than Springhill, schools nearer to the rink. Paul has never liked Springhill and, to be honest, it's never done much for him. I have talked to Paul about this and he has promised that he will work hard and that there will be no more complaints provided that he can move."

"Other schools?" Mr Crispin gaped, "What are you talking about? Springhill is his school. We chose it."

"We chose it because it was near here, Tony, not because it was the best school in the world. Well, now Paul needs to be somewhere else, so we pick the best school in that area. We might even consider boarding. I see no problem."

"No *problem*?" Mr Crispin yapped. "No problem? What are you talking about. You are proposing to upset Paul's education, turn the whole of our lives upside down, merely in order to enable him to mess around on ice? Madness! Madness!"

It took two more hours that night, three more days and nights of sulking, scenes and screaming-matches, before some semblance of peace was restored and Tony Crispin was prepared even to look at the school prospectuses which his wife placed before him at the breakfast-table. She knew her enemy, however, and, by reciting lists of distinguished politicians and soldiers who had attended King Edward's, Clapham, at last persuaded him to visit the school.

The headmaster, a retired major, expressed himself delighted to take on a pupil who happened to be a promising young skater, and undertook to "keep Paul's nose to the grindstone", the sort of expression that Tony Crispin liked. Two weeks later, in the middle of term, Paul attended King Edward's for the first time.

It was a grand, gothic, municipal sort of building of giant halls and echoing corridors lined with wooden boards recalling heroes of the past. To Paul's astonishment, he rapidly discovered himself to be popular. He was something of a curiosity, of course, which helped, and he did not, as at Springhill, carry the legacy of his early, ill-tempered years before skating had given him strength and confidence.

One boy in particular rapidly became his friend. Steve McCall was fair, good-looking and funny. He had a cheeky disrespect for authority, for games, for physical strength, and somehow always seemed to get away with murder.

Soon Paul and Steve were firm friends. Paul was

enchanted by the older boy's impudent charm. Some of Steve's talkativeness rubbed off on him. At the rink one evening in November, Anna and he were practising their Tango when suddenly Paul started to murmur, "Oh, God, but you are so beautiful, you are like the sleek jaguar that lurks in the jungle, the last star that lingers in the dawn sky. I feel your heart pound against mine, your slender body warm and vibrant in my arms . . ."

Anna stopped and wrenched herself free of his grasp, "What are you talking about?" she snapped.

"I – nothing," Paul laughed nervously. "Just a joke, that's all."

"Yeah, well keep your silly little boy jokes to yourself, will you? You're becoming a bore with all your stupid jokes. All the time, it's talk, talk, talk. I want to skate, right? So either you take it seriously or go home and let me get on with it, OK?"

"OK," Paul blinked, "keep your hair on. It was just a joke . . ."

Until now, Bunin had allowed them to enter no competitions. "You both know what competition is like," he said. "You both know how to behave on the big occasion. There's no purpose in making fools of yourselves at the bottom of the league. When we start, we start near the top."

Now, however, he declared them to be ready.

He mapped out their progress very carefully. Their first engagement would be in the Courtney Jones Trophy at Queen's, then just five more contests – at Nottingham, Solihull, Bristol and Southampton – before flying to Germany for the Fuji Film Cup and returning for the British Junior Dance Championships at Nottingham the following November. "Which," Bunin said laconically, "I expect you to win."

Paul's patience and perfectionism had contributed largely to the speed with which the pair had perfected the basic dances from which Compulsory Dances would be drawn. Several of these too had been worked up into Original Set Pattern dances. The free programme, choreographed by Bunin, was exuberant, comical and very, very hard work.

Once again, like Anna's solo programme, it was based upon a musical – this time, *Singin' in the Rain*. Paul was to wear loose cut white flannels, a cricket pullover and a white shirt with the sleeves rolled up, Anna a white sailor costume. The programme consisted of a brisk rumba to *Good Morning*, a dreamy Yankee polka to *You Were Meant for Me* and an exuberant, crash-bang-wallop Charleston to *All I Do is Dream of You*.

It was an absurdly ambitious programme, as Bunin admitted. "If it goes wrong," he said, "it will go very wrong. If it goes right, you will win." As he secretly confided to Gabriella over dinner at a *bistro* in Battersea Park Road, "They are both ambitious, both impatient. They respond better to a big challenge than to a small one. If I give them something easy to do, they make a mess of it. Just once, they have to do this absolutely right. Maybe it is on the night of the national championships, maybe not."

"And if not?"

"If not?" Bunin shrugged. "If not, they will not be noticed, admired, and I will be blamed for being a monster who pushed them too hard."

"You don't mind?"

"Me? No, I like that reputation. It helps. It means that star-struck mothers keep away from me."

"You can't accuse me of being one of those," Gabriella grinned.

"No, indeed. I never saw anyone less impressed by my overtures. I thought that you might hit me."

"I nearly did," Gabriella thoughtfully sliced her steak, then looked up at him over the candle at the centre of the red gingham tablecloth. "Tell me . . ." she started, then stopped.

"Tell you what?"

"Would you have started with Anna . . . ?"

"If I hadn't seen you and liked what I saw?" Bunin raised his eyebrows. "Oh, yes. It was a happy coincidence, that is all – or maybe not such a coincidence that a beautiful mother should have a daughter with Anna's confidence and fire."

Gabriella looked down at her plate again. "So she's really good?"

"Oh yes, she's really good, but don't tell her that I said so. She is – slapdash I think is the word – but that is because she is brave and romantic and throws herself into her skating. That is why I chose Paul. He works hard. He is very serious, very careful. If Anna can pick up a little of Paul's technique and Paul can pick up some of Anna's – Anna's 'oomph', they will be a great pair."

"Skating seems to reflect real life," Gabriella dabbed her lips with a napkin and pushed her plate away. "Anna is all 'oomph' and Paul is all serious hard work. I wish she would stop sometimes and think a little too."

"It will come," Bunin waved to a waiter. "It will come. She is growing and learning. So is Paul. But there will be many arguments, many disappointments, many tragedies before – well, you and I both know what I mean."

"Yes," said Gabriella quietly. "I know what you mean."

"Win or lose, though," said Bunin gravely, "This will be good for Anna and for Paul. Your work and money are not wasted."

"Oh. I need to hear that every day of the week." Gabriella leaned back as the waiter picked up her plate. She stretched. "Especially when I have to get up at five o'clock every morning to feed the creature and then have to scrub the floors of the idle rich all day."

"You cook for her in the mornings?" Bunin frowned.

"Yes, of course."

"Very well. I do not train her any more."

"What are you talking about?"

"Skating is not just about what happens on ice," Bunin said sternly. "If she cares enough to be good, she cooks her own breakfast."

"But she's never . . ." Gabriella stared, "I mean, she works hard enough already."

"Make up your mind," Bunin said crisply. "Either she gets up, cooks breakfast – and I mean a proper cooked breakfast – and makes her way to the rink without disturbing you, or I do not train her."

"Now, wait a minute, Mister Bunin," Gabriella threw her napkin down on to the table. "You are in charge of Anna when she is skating. I am her mother and I decide how I run my home."

"Of course you do," Bunin smiled sweetly, "and you have a simple decision to make. Either way you will not have to get up at five o'clock any more."

"I have always looked after my own child, thank you, and I intend to continue to do so."

"Splendid, then both of you can lie in every morning." Bunin bowed, "Pudding?"

"No, thank you," Gabriella hissed. "I would like to go home, thank you."

Once out on the street, Gabriella vented her full fury on Bunin. He nodded, smiled and agreed with her all the way home as she told him what she thought of him.

At the Robilliard Estate, she rapped out a quick, "And good night!" and ran up the staircase. Bunin heard the thrumming of her feet on the walkway, the bang as the door slammed shut. He smiled ruefully and sauntered off with lazy grace to find a bus.

"Have a good breakfast?" he asked Anna when he stepped on to the ice at eight o'clock the following morning.

Her nose wrinkled up. She grinned, "Disgusting."

"Eggs?"

"And bacon, and tomatoes and bread and cereal and orange-juice. The cereal and the orange-juice weren't burned."

Bunin laughed. "You'll learn."

"Yeah, I know. I've been telling Gabi for years not to get up. She was furious last night. Thinks you're a filthy pig and quite a lot of worse things and she's never going to talk to you again."

"Hey ho," Bunin hummed, "I'll live. Now," he clapped once, loudly, "any problems?"

"So, what are you up to tonight, Paul?" Steve leaned back in his chair, his feet on the desk. He combed his fair hair back with his fingers, then turned back to flicking casually through *Sunday Sport*.

"Skating, of course," Paul replied, surprised.

"Boring!" Steve sang. "You want to watch it, you know. You could turn into a fish finger, spending so long on the ice."

"Ha ha." He did not look up from his struggle with the logarithm tables.

"No, but seriously, mate, it's not natural. You should get out a bit, meet a few girls, learn about the real world."

"Yeah, well," Paul frowned irritably, "one day. When I'm world champion."

"When you're dead, more like. I mean, look, you're free as a flamin' bird, mate! Your parents think you're skating. We could go down the West End, have a few drinks, pull a few girls, have a real good time. I mean, I'm serious about this. It can't be good for you, cut off from the world, thinking of nothing but skating, for Christ's sakes. People go do-lally when they do things like that. It's medical fact. Nature always wins through in the end, and if you've been bottling things up, they explode with a bang. You're a fit young male animal. You ever feel like exploding?"

Paul looked up from his exercise book and smiled shyly. "Sometimes," he admitted.

"Yeah, well, there you are! You've got to get some experience of life! I mean, one day you're going to look round and half your life'll be gone and you'll realize you've done nothing. I mean, sure, you'll be better at skating than anyone, but a fat lot of good that'll do you when your youth's gone and there's no more skating and you've never gone out with a girl, never got tight, never done a single thing guys our age are meant to do. Jeez, I mean, you might die tomorrow . . ."

"Shut up, Steve," Paul spoke sulkily. The thought was never far from his mind. He did not need reminding.

"Look, how old's this Italian girl you dance with?"

"Fourteen."

"That's what I mean! There's you, every day, handling all that toothsome jailbait – and those eyeties, I know what they're like, mate, and you get to look but not touch. It's enough to drive a saint to drink! I'm serious. It worries me. You'll skate better too, get a bit of experience, I bet you. Gor." He opened the paper and carefully chose his favourite model. Stabbing the picture with his forefinger he added, "Tell the truth mate, rather be there than an ice-rink, wouldn't you?"

"Yeah, maybe," Paul's husky laugh was nervous, "but you don't get those walking about every street."

"Don't you just?" Steve swung his feet from the table and leaned forward, resting his forearms on Paul's desk. "Just you follow your uncle Steve, kid. Just come with me for one evening. I'll show you."

"I can't!" Paul almost wailed, "I've got the competition at Queen's on Saturday!"

"Not a nancy boy are you, Paul?" Steve asked casually.

"Get lost," Paul snarled.

"Quite sure? I mean, I'm not prejudiced or anything, and lots of these dancing and skating guys are woofters, so I'm told."

"Get lost I said," Paul pushed Steve's arms off the desk.

"All right, all right." Steve stood with a broad grin and strolled over to the window. "Tell you what," he said suddenly, "one day next week. You can afford just one evening, can't you? Can't make that much difference to your skating, but, boy, what a difference it'll make to you."

Paul did not look up from his writing. Steve shrugged, sighed and flapped his hand dismissively. "I give up," he said. He walked towards the door. "I've done my very best . . ."

"We'll see," Paul said quietly. "After the competition, let's see."

Paul clambered from a taxi on Wandsworth High Road and puffed out a lot of steam as he thanked the driver and paid him. The taxi throbbed and shuddered and moved off. Paul shuddered back at it. Despite the warmth of his scarf and long tweed overcoat, the cold seeped up his sleeves and trickled down his collar.

He picked up his overnight bag and crossed the road to the wire fence surrounding the Robilliard Estate. He scanned the ragged buildings. Dusk gathered in the doorways. Five black children slouched against the wall, ghetto-blaster blaring. A very old woman wheeled a pushchair across the forecourt through empty coke cans and scuttling paper bags. Paul followed her.

He trotted up the stairs of Verulam House. National Front graffiti wavered before his eyes on every landing. There was a strong smell of urine in the stairwell. He was glad to be out again in the open air on the walkway.

He did not need to knock on the Lombardi's door, for Anna was at the sink overlooking the walkway. She waved and smiled and pulled off her rubber gloves. Paul waited while she came round to the front door.

He saw her blurred approach as though underwater through the frosted glass. The door swung inward. She smiled warmly at him. "Hi."

"Hi." He grinned. He was so accustomed to seeing her in practice costume with her hair up that her appearance here in a simple calf length scarlet cotton dress, her hair swept back by a black velvet band tumbling loosely over her shoulders, startled him. She looked at once younger and more feminine. On the ice he was inclined to forget that she was a girl.

"Come on in," she stepped back. "It's freezing out there."

"I know," he followed her down the passage. "Are you all ready for tomorrow?"

"Don't ask," she laughed over her shoulder. She turned left and led him into the living-room.

"Paul!" Gabriella got up from behind her desk. Much to his surprise, she ignored his outstretched hand and kissed him. She smelt good. Her skin was very warm against Paul's cheek. He blushed. In her white lacy shirt, black waistcoat and black jeans, she wasn't quite as mothers should be. "Take off your coat," she said, "drop that case. Sit down."

Paul obeyed orders, though not in the order specified. He had to fetch the bottle of wine and the box of chocolates from his case before removing his coat, searching for a hook and at last sitting on one of the black leather chairs.

He was up and out of it again almost immediately when Gabriella came in with three glasses and a corkscrew and placed them on the table. "Will you pour the wine?" she asked cheerfully.

"Er – yes, of course." Paul had little experience of using a corkscrew, but he disguised his nervousness as best he could. "I hope it's OK," he said, "the wine, I mean. I thought Italian was a good idea and the man in the shop said it was good . . ."

"*Dolcetto*," Gabriella nodded. "It comes from Piemonte. It is a beautiful mountainous part of Italy with very fine fungus and very fine wine and food."

A little giggle forced its way from Paul's throat as he poured wine into Gabriella's glass.

"What's so funny?" she laughed.

"Fungus, mama," Anna sighed. "You always forget it's 'mushrooms' in English."

"Oh – sorry, Paul. Yes. Anna is right. Lots of different sorts of mushrooms. Anna and me, we were there four years ago. You remember Dronero, Anna? We drank Dolcetto there. Thank you, Paul," she smiled up at him and took the glass, "but what about Anna? And you? You do not like wine?"

"Er . . . oh," said Paul intelligently. At home, he would never have thought of pouring himself wine, nor would anyone have dreamed of offering it to him, still less to Anna. He was astonished by the naturalness with which Anna took the offered glass and drank.

His astonishment was to increase all evening. On his arrival, he had had, he realized, some vague preconceptions about life in a small Wandsworth flat and, indeed, about life in an Italian one parent family. He had thought, perhaps that he was more sophisticated, better acquainted with the good things in life.

Tonight he learned otherwise. He was expected, he discovered, to keep the two women's glasses filled and to light Gabriella's cigarettes. The food was simple but delicious – *gnocchi* – little green balls of spinach and cream cheese in melted butter and sprinkled with parmesan, *bollito*, beef boiled until it was glutinous and flaky, served with a cold green sauce that tasted of parsley, anchovies and capers, then a salad, then cheese without bread or biscuits but eaten, he discovered, on its own with a few drops of thick green olive oil.

Conversation too was very different from that to which he was accustomed at home. Over dinner, coffee and the washing up, politics, food, architecture, sex, education and, of course, skating, were discussed. Paul was surprised to discover that he was expected to have opinions and to express them. Such a thing had never happened at home, where theoretical talk occurred only between adults and even then seemed always to be dominated by personal one-upmanship.

The wine, the food, the female company, the flattering sense that he was someone of importance, at first made him confident and talkative, then happy and mellow, then, as they sat in the living-room chatting about tomorrow's contest, very sleepy. Three or four times, his eyelids sank and his vision grew hazy and he had to shake his head and force himself to listen to something that someone was saying. At the last, he gave up the unequal struggle and sank contentedly into the darkness.

"Come on, Paul, time for bed." He opened his eyes. The lights had been turned out, the coffee cleared away. The only light came from the kitchen. Gabriella bent over him. Her hair touched her smile, his cheek.

He smiled goofily back at her. "Sorry," he croaked, "I dozed off."

"Don't worry. We've made up the bed. Here." She gestured towards the corner of the room where a zed-bed stood beneath the window. It looked very inviting. Paul staggered over to it and, while Gabriella and Anna talked quietly in the kitchen, quickly undressed and clambered in. Somewhere way below, the waves of traffic broke and receded. Distant footfalls clattered. Somewhere too there was music, though you could hear nothing but the fizzing bass.

"Goodnight, Paul." Gabriella called.

"'Night."

Cotton rustled. Bare feet padded on the carpet. He turned his head. Anna stood above the bed. The dim light from the window made her long white nightdress appear ghostly blue, whilst her hair had a wispy white aura in the light from the kitchen. "Here," she said, "hot chocolate." She squatted down and placed the steaming mug on the carpet, then stood again.

"Thank you." Paul blinked up at her.

"'Night, Paul," she bent quickly and lightly kissed his

lips, then straightened, turned and walked away. Her left arm arose in the oblong of light. The light snapped off.

Paul's fingers touched his lips. "Goodnight, Anna," he murmured, and lay back with a smile and a sigh.

The mug of chocolate was still full when he awoke at the shrilling of Anna's alarm clock. He jumped from bed. It was still dark. The sky outside was black as silver, but already someone had started work with the Goddards at the horizon. Paul shivered and dressed rapidly. All his thoughts now were on the competition ahead.

Anna bustled through the room on her way to the bathroom. She whispered "Good morning" and was gone. She too was already rehearsing in her mind each movement of the free routine.

Paul stripped the bed. The bath water thudded and growled. Next door, Gabriella's bed creaked as she too got up. She padded through to the kitchen in her dressing gown, hair all over her face, and afforded Paul a little wave as she passed. The strip-light blinked. She blinked back at it. She put the coffee pot on the stove and returned to her bedroom to dress.

Ten minutes later, everyone was in the kitchen. Paul was polishing the skates. Anna and Gabriella were preparing breakfast. When they spoke, for some reason, it was in whispers. There was a lot of excited giggling. When at last the taxi arrived and they set off down the stairs, laden with costumes, skates, towels, Carmen rollers, make-up and Paul's overnight bag, the sky was marbled grey like a washstand top.

"Queen's Ice Rink, please," Paul told the taxi-driver, "in Queensway."

* * *

"Must we really go, Mummy?" Katie Crispin whined. "I mean, I have got better things to do."

"Such as?"

"Well, I've got to ring Caroline."

"Caroline who? All your friends are called Caroline."

"Caroline Vane, Mummy," Katie sighed tolerantly. "Don't be silly. I'm meant to be staying with her in Devon this week for her party, remember? And anyhow, all my friends aren't called Caroline. There's Emma and Camilla . . ."

"And Ermintrude and Esmerelda," said Mrs Crispin drily. "Well, yes, dear, I'm afraid I think that watching your brother at his first big ice-dance competition is rather more important than exchanging bitchy gossip with Wilhelmina."

"Caroline!"

"What? Oh, yes. Even your father's coming with something like good grace, so I shall expect you to be radiating goodwill and looking nice in . . ." she looked at her watch, "just forty-five minutes from now, OK?"

"OK," Katie groaned. Her feet clattered and scraped as she slouched from the room.

Mrs Crispin sighed. She stirred the simmering soup on the stove and walked to the back door. "Tony!" she called, and her breath bounced back at her off the icy air. "Tony! Come on! Time to change!"

Bunin, Gabriella, Anna and Paul were eating pizzas just a hundred yards down the road when the crowds started arriving for the competition. All afternoon, Anna and Paul had wanted to return to the ice, but Bunin had forbidden it. After four hours' work this morning in which they accustomed themselves to the different ice texture and size of the rink, practised the compulsory figures –

Starlight Waltz, Argentine Tango and Blues – and ran through the free programme without mishap but with much habitual bickering, their trainer had insisted that they should relax. *Bambi* had been re-released for Christmas, so, reluctantly at first, they had suffered themselves to be led to the cinema.

Bunin had never seen the film before. He and Gabriella were captivated from the outset. Anna and Paul sat straight-backed and fumed for a few minutes, but it could not last for long. Paul started laughing first. Anna was totally engrossed a few seconds later. It was the adults however whose eyes were wet with tears when at last they emerged on to Marble Arch. It had been raining. The roads were dazzling. People scampered homeward, hunched over their parcels and carrier-bags. Anna and Paul, of course, instantly wanted to return to the rink, but Bunin calmly led them to the Pizza Parlour. Paul and Anna continually looked up at the clock as they ate, but Bunin chatted happily to Gabriella and ignored them.

When at last they arrived at the rink again, it was already half past five. "Plenty of time to change and have a warm up," Bunin announced, but only Gabriella heard him. Paul and Anna were already half-way to the changing-rooms.

They did not look up at the audience when first they came out on to the ice in their plain black costumes. They were too busy assessing the competition. They recognized a few of the couples. Helen Swann and Mark Piper skated at Richmond. Mark had taken his Inter-Silver figures-and-free at the same time as Paul.

Cliff Owen and Sandra Bailey were known to them only by sight. They had been second in last year's British Juniors and were expected to win this year. Both were seventeen and had been skating together for four years.

They skated about the rink with the smug, arrogant air of old-boys returning to their old school. Cliff had terraced red hair. Sandra was blonde and had very red lips. Paul irrationally disliked them on sight.

Unlike them, Paul and Anna did not warm up together. They skated alone, just getting the feel of the ice without the restrictive responsibility of a partner. They also took the opportunity to show off their exceptional individual skills. Sandra Bailey and Cliff Owen, for example, had never been figure-skaters. Few dancers had. When Paul and Anna threw themselves into jumps and spins therefore, the others watched in intimidated awe or, in Bailey and Owen's case, looked the other way and pretended that it was not happening.

Only when the warm-up period was over did Paul and Anna have a chance to scan the seats around the rink. Gabriella and Bunin sat together at the front. It was obvious from the small approving smile on Gabriella's face that she understood what Anna and Paul were doing, and why.

The Crispins sat with Mrs Mottistone at the other end of the rink. Paul waved at them as he left the ice. Mr and Mrs Crispin waved back. Mrs Crispin smiled. Katie yawned very obviously.

"Good evening, ladies and gentlemen," the loudspeaker declared, "and welcome to Queen's. Tonight we see the very best of our young ice dancers, the champions of tomorrow, in the Queen's Cup Junior Ice Dance Open Championships. Just a brief word of explanation to those who don't know the score. Each of these young couples will skate three compulsory figures, the Starlight Waltz, the Argentine Tango and the Blues. These represent 30 per cent of the total marks. Then they will do an Original Set Pattern Dance to the Viennese Waltz with fifty-seven to sixty-three bars per minute in three-four time. These represent 20 per cent of the total. And last, they will do their own thing in a free dance of four minutes' duration which, as the mathematicians amongst you will have worked out, represents the remaining 50 per cent. In your programmes, you will find the names of the competitors and a scoresheet on which you record the scores awarded by each judge. So! Let's get on with the action. And the first competitors, all the way from Nottingham, are Trevor Bayliss and Mary Daneman!"

The compulsory figures went well for Paul and Anna. At the end, Bunin just nodded and announced, "Good tracings." The judges placed them second to Bailey and Owen. "Sheep," Bunin snorted in the direction of the judges.

"I told you they were better," Katie did a little seated dance. "They were second in the National Championships, it says here."

"Well, I thought they were OK," Mrs Crispin mused, "but Anna and Paul were much more – vigorous, much more attractive. Those two, Bailey and Owen, they were – I don't know – prissy."

"I agree, actually," Tony Crispin drawled. "No verve. Quite impressed, really, by Paul and thingy, I mean. Stupid sport of course, but still." He paused for a while then turned with a quick grin as quickly effaced, "Least it's not synchronized swimming."

"You were good," Paul said stiffly.

"Thanks a lot." Anna laughed without humour. "We're not going to win though. That Sandra and Cliff are good. Much smoother than we are."

"I know," Paul nodded slowly, "but we're not doing badly. We've got a long way to go, that's all. Let's practise that sequence after the stag lift, shall we?"

"OK," Anna stretched, "but for God's sake keep your leg up this time."

"Keep your head down, more like," Paul retorted . . .

It was impossible to say at what point things started to go wrong in the Set Pattern Dance, or who was responsible. Paul was convinced afterwards that Anna had wavered on an outside leg, had thrust out an arm to prevent herself from falling and everything had gone wrong from then on. Anna maintained that the problem started a second earlier and that Paul had thrown her off balance with his weight. Either way, once things went out of synch, they became progressively worse.

There were no obvious disasters, no falls, no stumbles. To the inexpert eyes of most of the audience, it was a competent performance. To Paul and Anna, however, it was a disaster.

They were astonished by the warm applause of the audience at the end and by the marks which the judges awarded. The marks for composition were good enough to keep them in second place overall. The marks for presentation, quite rightly, knocked them down to third.

"Not so good?" Gabriella asked a grim-faced Bunin.

"Not so good," he said dully. "Still, I did not expect miracles. They are just starting. Another four, five years and . . ." he shrugged.

"And?" Gabriella prompted.

"They may be good."

"Have to be patient in this game, don't you?"

"It seems that way," Bunin nodded, "until your skating career is over and then it seems that it has all just taken a moment. They have perhaps ten years. Not long out of a life. But yes. Ten years of pain and injury and hard work and patience. And don't forget. At the moment they are aiming to beat the British Junior champions. That may take a year, it may take two. Then suddenly they meet all the other young skaters from all over the world, all of them as good as Paul and Anna, many much, much better. They triumph there perhaps, and move into the seniors. Again they beat the other British skaters. Still they have to beat the world. Then at last they are world champions, Olympic champions. They turn professional and they are babies all over again, only half as good as professionals who no one has heard of who do cabarets and ice shows. The chances of getting there, you will see, are infinitesimal, like the chances of man developing from the first organism. But – who knows? – it happens sometimes. Once in a lifetime, it happens."

"It happened to you," said Gabriella.

"Oh, yes, it happened to me, but standards have changed. In two, three years' time, I will have nothing to teach them. They will be better than I ever was and still they will merely be Olympic possibles. I have experience. I know a lot about making good precise figures and beautiful tracings. That is all."

"So who trains them then?"

"No one," Bunin shook his head. "They train themselves. I will be there, of course, to push them, to perfect this or that detail that they have not seen, but that is all."

"And now," Bunin tore his eyes from hers, "I must go and see our young prodigies. I think they will need kicking a bit."

* * *

"Oh, go away!" Anna yapped and turned towards the foyer wall, "I don't want to listen to you any more, I don't want to see you any more, I don't want to skate with you any more. You're pathetic. You can't even admit when you've made a mistake."

"I admit when I've made a mistake, all right," Paul

grasped her shoulder and tried to spin her around but she pulled away with a shrill yelp of anger. "But I didn't make a mistake this time. It was when you wobbled on that turn! You damned nearly knocked my eye out."

"Shut up, shut up, shut up!" Anna clenched her fist and her whole body trembled. She swung around. Snail tracks of tears glistened on her cheeks. Her eyes were wild. "I never want to skate with you again! I will find someone else. You, anyhow, are dead from the neck down, dead, dead, dead! No wonder we will never win. You have the passion of a fish!"

He felt the warm puffs of breath on his lips as she flung the words at him. "Oh," he said through gritted teeth, "so I've the passion of a fish, have I?" His eyes narrowed. Colour arose into his cheeks. He took one step towards her. "Well you just listen, Miss brilliant Lombardi . . ."

She stepped backward. He followed.

"You are both pathetic," Bunin's voice rang in the walls. Paul and Anna span around. Bunin emerged slowly from the shadows into the dim light at the centre of the foyer. "You are both children," he said, "and it is I, not you, who will break up this partnership. You do not deserve that I should teach you. First you skate badly, then you behave badly. I do not teach babies like that."

"But . . ." Anna began.

"No buts, thank you, Anna. You skated like – like a pudding. Something went wrong and you became useless, and then you blame Paul. You are spoiled, vain, stupid and over-emotional. I do not know why I ever agreed to teach you. You have wasted a great deal of my valuable time."

"That's not fair," Paul stepped forward, still flushed.

"I am coming to you, Paul," Bunin snarled. "You are the technician here. You are meant to have some control over your movements on ice, even if Anna has none. You had a responsibility to pick the performance up, to lead the dance. You failed. I am disappointed in you. You obviously have not the qualities necessary in a good skater. You are a coward, and you too, like Anna, seek to blame someone else for the action of the fates. I will explain to your parents on Monday morning."

"But, Mr Bunin," Anna blurted as the tears started to flow again. "Please! Paul didn't . . ."

"That is enough," Bunin said curtly. "Do your free dance, and that will be that." He turned on his heel and strode from the room.

"But – but that's not *fair*!" Anna whispered as she watched him go. "All we did was . . . all we did was make a mistake, and . . . and . . ." A silent sob shook her shoulders.

Paul laid a hand on her upper arm and gently squeezed. "I don't know what's come over him," he frowned. "You don't think he really means not to train us any more, do you?"

"I don't know," Anna wailed. "I – I don't know. I didn't understand."

"He can't just stop because of a little thing like this. He can't! And the things he said about you. I mean, they were so unfair!"

"And about you," Anna gulped. "I'm – I'm sorry, Paul."

"So am I," Paul said glumly. "Well, I reckon it's time we changed . . ."

"Why are you looking so pleased with yourself?" Gabriella turned with laughing eyes as Bunin resumed his seat beside her.

"Because I have just been brutal and unfair and have

insulted both Paul and your daughter in the most disgusting way."

"Oh, that's good. What did you say?"

"I told Anna that she skated like a pudding. I have never seen a pudding skate, but she seemed a little affronted. I told Paul that he was a coward. I did my best to imply that I would not teach them any more."

"But *why*?" Gabriella demanded.

"Because they were not a couple on the ice, because they were bickering and accusing one another afterwards. If you have two small enemies and one big one turns up and attacks them both, what happens?"

"The two small ones unite," Gabriella laughed. "Poor Anna."

"So now they have a motive to please me and they are very close together. That is good," Bunin said smugly.

"But what about the comedy at the end? They're hardly going to be funny if they are in floods of tears."

"No. Perhaps not," Bunin mused. "I will have to think of something. Let's wait and see."

Paul and Anna knew that they could not win. They also knew that they had nothing to lose. Bailey and Owen were unassailable after an impeccable if unadventurous free programme, and this might be the last time that Crispin and Lombardi would ever skate together in competition. All that they cared about now was showing Bunin what they thought of him and his opinions.

There was a ripple of applause as they skated to the centre of the ice to begin the free dance. After all the sequin encrusted costumes of the other competitors, Paul's plain white flannels and Anna's crisp white sailor-suit were startlingly fresh and original.

Afterwards, Paul and Anna were not to recall a single

thing about the *Good Morning* section. They knew that the crowd started clapping in time with the music and that on several occasions there were uniform gasps and bursts of applause, but otherwise it seemed that they had switched off their conscious brains. They responded to the months of training as though to the click of a hypnotist's fingers. Each note of music engendered a pre-programmed response. They were unified by total concentration on a single aim.

It felt good.

In *You Were Meant For Me*, Paul, perhaps for the first time, threw himself body and soul into a character. He loved this girl into whose wide, tear-blurred eyes he gazed. He wanted her and these people all around to know it, but he was dumb. He had to act it out with his eyes, his hands, his whole body. When, it seemed, she understood and returned his love, he closed his eyes in sheer delight and skipped triumphantly into a mad, double time polka, raising her up time and again so that he could feast his eyes upon her, rushing to take her into his arms again each time that she drew away. Neither of them actually thought about a single technical problem throughout the dance.

At the end, Anna curtsied low while Paul bowed over her, her outstretched hand to his lips. There was absolute silence throughout the rink, then the raucous notes of *All I Do is Dream of You* blazed out, and suddenly the significance of their positions changed. He was asking her to dance. The only problem was that he did not know how to Charleston. The idea was that she would try to teach him, he would stumble and flounder in his bid to copy her and they would end with a very fast, very complicated dance when at last he got the message.

Anna left the centre of the rink first, dragging Paul

behind her. She skated directly towards Bunin and Gabriella. As she neared the end of the rink, Bunin stood. He smiled broadly. He clapped. First Anna saw him, then Paul as they sped past, and suddenly there was a new gleam in Anna's eyes as imperiously she whirled Paul round into a spin.

It was not just Bunin who was smiling and clapping ninety seconds later as the routine drew to its close. Bunin had worked hard to make this section funny and explosive. He had succeeded. Paul was discovering for the first time the joys of making people laugh, and the breakneck speed at which he and Anna completed their final two circuits of the rink left everyone in the house breathless.

The applause at the end sounded like the roar of air in the ear of a surfacing swimmer. Paul and Anna blinked and smiled and looked startled, as though they had just been awoken to find themselves in a strange and beautiful place. They were allowed to skate off the rink just as the judges' marks were read out over the tannoy. "And the marks for technical merit for Anna Lombardi and Paul Crispin . . ."

Paul squeezed Anna's hand. Together they stood wide-eyed as the marks were read out. For technical merit, they were exceptionally high, for artistic impression they were astronomical, outstripping Bailey and Owen by more than half a point, outstripping any marks that they had ever heard of at this level.

"There," Bunin's voice close behind them was casual, "you see what can be done if you put your minds to it. It felt good, hm?"

"Wonderful," Anna grinned, "as though I'd been wearing diver's boots all my life until then."

"And suddenly you knew that you couldn't make a mistake?" Bunin smiled, "And that if Paul did something out of the ordinary you would adapt without thinking?" She nodded. "I know the feeling," he said, "and the audience recognizes it. You are lucky. Now you know what we are looking for. You cannot decide when it will happen. Sometimes it is there, sometimes not. The more you work, the more often it will come. It is a great lesson. You do not matter any more. You submit. You are a servant to the dance. It is good."

Paul looked at his feet, then up at Bunin, "Er, what you said earlier . . ."

"I meant every word," said Bunin stiffly, "I was speaking then to two very stupid children. If I see them again, I shall say the same. Tonight's free dance was good only because those children were no longer about. It was good because something exceptional happened to both of you and you became, for the first time, a pair. It was not good because either or both of you is brilliant. You are slightly above average junior ice-dancers. Do not forget it." He looked at his watch. "I will see you on Monday morning," he announced. "Good night."

The door banged behind him. Anna and Paul both sighed at the same moment, "I could come to hate that man," Paul growled, but a smile touched his lips.

"Me too," Anna yawned luxuriously. "Me too."

* * *

"Not bad, son. Really not bad at all. Most impressed." Tony Crispin's face was alternately splashed with yellow light then sunk in blackness as he steered the car down the ramp of the dark multi-storey car park. "Good little girl, too, that Italian."

"Well, I thought they were brilliant. Really really." June Crispin turned in the passenger seat to smile at Paul. "Much better than those two that won."

"No," Paul said equably, "they deserved to win. They were more disciplined."

"Yes," Mr Crispin nodded, "but I must say, they were rather boring. You two, well, I quite enjoyed watching your bit," he sounded astonished.

"Wasn't bad," Katie sniffed, "but those girls! I don't know how you can stand it, Paul. I mean, every one of them, plastered with cheap make-up and waggling their big bums and giggling. I mean, you never get to meet anyone normal in that world. I'd go mad. And all they can talk about is skating. They don't know anything about the real world."

"They're not all like that," Paul's voice was flat. "In fact very few of them are."

"Oh, come on!" Katie groaned, "I saw them, Paul. They're not exactly sophisticated, are they? I mean, look at your little friend. She's got no *idea*. Most of the boys are wet, too. You can see it."

"My little friend," Paul said slowly, "knows a great deal more about how to behave than you. She is more intelligent than you, better mannered than you and, as a matter of interest, considerably better-looking than you."

Katie gasped. "How dare you!" she gave a suppressed shriek, then decided that condescending laughter would serve her better. "Oh, just listen!" she sang, "Just listen to little Paulie talking absolute unmitigated gibberish! Poor Paulie, are you besotted with your silly little Italian bit? Oh, just listen, Paul's in love, Mummy."

"I am not," Paul snapped. Hot needles pricked his cheeks.

"Or maybe Paulie's just wet like the others," Katie continued with savagery.

"That's enough, Katie," her father ordered.

"Yes," Mrs Crispin said decisively, "you're both being

very silly. You shouldn't be so cruel to Katie, Paul, and you, Katie, shouldn't be a snob."

There was silence from the back of the car then for four or five minutes. "Mind you," Tony Crispin's voice broke the silence, "Katie has got a point, you know. You really should get to meet some people – girls and things – in normal sorts of social situations. It can't be good to limit yourself. You're growing up, you know. Time you started learning about the world outside. Have to see what we can do about it, eh, June?"

"Yes, I suppose so," said Mrs Crispin. "It is true that skating is a very small world."

"They're all morons," said Katie.

"Time you got yourself a bit of experience of the world," mused Mr Crispin.

"Time for a drink, I reckon," Steve pushed open the cinema doors and sauntered on to the street. Paul followed. Slush crunched beneath their feet. It was late February. The streets reflected the flashing lights above strip clubs, cinema clubs and sex shops.

"Didn't think much of that," Paul said glumly, "I mean, you didn't see anything"

"Ah, no, my old pal, but that's 'cos of the censorship, see," Steve turned into Archer Street. "I mean, they were really doing it, and in the old days you'd have seen the lot, but they've cut all the good bits out these days. Spoilsports."

This was the fifth time that Paul had skived off skating practice for a trip to Soho with Steve. They smoked, drank, watched movies, visited strip clubs and video booths and played the machines at the amusement arcades. Each time, Paul had returned home feeling lousy. Each time he had wished that he had gone to the ice-rink instead. Each time he vowed that he would not accompany Steve again. Each time that Steve suggested another "night on the town", he went.

The guilt and the disillusion seemed to last only so long before the excitement of anticipation banished them. It was not the dingy clubs that he craved but the sense of adventure. It was exciting and frightening to walk these streets, to be treated like an adult, to enter forbidden territories, to watch the hustlers, the gamblers, the pimps, the drunks and the punters going about their business. To Paul as to many mug-punters, the squalor of these lives seemed exotic, the savour of forbidden fruit delicious, no matter how bad it made him feel afterwards.

Bunin had objected, of course, and Anna had kicked up a stink when Paul did not turn up at the rink, but what did they think he was, an automaton? Steve was right. Mr Crispin was right. There had to be life outside skating. And anyhow, Bunin had no cause to complain. The Crispins paid him generously enough and, in the three competitions in which they had skated, they had twice been second to Bailey and Owen and once, at Southampton, when Bailey and Owen had not been there, had won. In the South of England at least, Lombardi and Crispin were already established as the second best junior ice-dance couple.

"There you go, mate," Steve placed four glasses on the table, "pint of bitter and a large Scotch. Only place where ice is any good to anyone, I reckon."

Anna had waited patiently at first. Paul, after all, could have been detained at school, or someone could have thrown himself in the path of his train. She had skated alone, taking the opportunity to practise some of her solo figures. Other skaters arrived. Tracey, now a rare visitor, skated over in a sheer green satin body stocking. "Where's lover boy, then?" she asked.

"Dunno," Anna replied, "held up, I suppose."

"Good. You can show me a few tricks then. Come on, cheer up, superspag. He'll be here soon."

Osbert Keevil arrived at seven o'clock in black stretch ski-pants and black polo-neck. He watched the two girls for a moment with a sly appreciative smile, then skated towards them, executed a high double selko and glided the last five yards on one knee, right arm extended towards Anna.

"All alone?" He did something with his face which only he would call a smile. "This is my lucky day."

"Not ours, greaseball," said Tracey succinctly.

"That's not pleasant," he raised an eyebrow in mock affront and stood, dusting his knee. "I have longed for the moment when I would find the lovely Miss Lombardi alone. Come, Anna, dance with me."

"Oh, go away!" Anna snapped.

"Osbert took two rapid steps backward. "I'm sorry," he said, then recovered his composure and bowed low, "I merely thought . . ."

"Shut up, will you?" Anna's voice faltered. Several heads turned. She swung round, covered her face with her hands and almost stumbled from the rink.

"What's up with her?" Osbert asked innocently.

"She's got taste," Tracey snapped and followed Anna up the ramp.

She found her sitting stiffly at a table in the cafeteria. You could clearly see the streaks across her temples where she had dashed away the tears. Now she was dry-eyed and her lips were a thin, straight scar.

"Old Osbert is weeping tears of pure oil," Tracey smiled. She pulled out a chair and sat astride it. "Come on, Annie, he'll be back tomorrow. Give yourself a night off too."

"We can't have nights off," Anna bit off the words and spat them out in foul tasting chunks. "We haven't got time."

"Oh, come on, it's not the end of the world, love. Relax. Come with me. We'll go down the bowling-alley or something. It'll do you good."

"I can't relax," Anna answered in a monotone. "If I'm not skating when I should be, I feel guilty. I can't enjoy myself."

"Force yourself."

"No, Tracey. I can't. Every hour that we miss – every minute – is cutting down our chances of taking the Juniors. We've got enough to do as it is, for God's sake. I mean, we're a *pair*. I depend on him making an effort. If he behaves like this, I suffer, not just him."

"I know," Tracey leaned forward and laid a hand on Anna's arm, "but you're getting too uptight about this. I know he's behaving like a twerp. I mean, the least the little runt could do is to let you know if he's going to skive, but one night isn't going to make that much difference."

"You don't understand," Anna said sadly. She turned and looked down at the rink, where Osbert skated alone. "I suppose I'd better go and say I'm sorry," she said.

"I shouldn't bother."

"Oh, he's not so bad. Bit flash, that's all," Anna stood. "At least he's reliable."

"Yeah, you can rely on him to be a pain in the backside, far as I'm concerned. Still, it's your funeral."

When Bunin arrived half an hour later, he found Anna and Osbert skating the Starlight Waltz together. Bunin said nothing. He just sat down by the side of the rink and watched.

At last he seemed to come to a decision. He stood, sighed and stepped on to the ice. "Anna," he beckoned, "no, and you," he pointed at Osbert, "come over here."

Anna skated up at once. Osbert followed a little nervously just a few yards behind. "What excuse did he give this time, Anna?" Bunin demanded in a low voice.

"None," she shrugged, "I haven't heard from him."

"Right," he nodded. "You. What is your name?"

"Osbert."

"Well, Osbert, you are holding Anna all wrong. Look carefully now . . . "

When Paul woke up the next morning with a headache and a mouthful of moths, he considered what story he should tell to excuse his absence. "I'm sorry, but one of the masters at school put me in detention," would not do. It was too easily checked, and did not explain why he did not telephone. "Something cropped up at home" or "My father insisted that I stay" or "My uncle came unexpectedly to dinner" had their merits, but he had used them before.

But as the train rattled up to Streatham and his headache grew worse, he became more and more resolved to tell the truth. He was a free agent, after all, and Bunin was his employee. No one could tell him how he should spend his time. He was not a child any more. He had given more time and effort to skating than most working men gave to their jobs, and if on occasion he felt like a day off, that was nobody's business but his own.

He swaggered into the club with a bullish expression on his face. He had his speech prepared.

He was never to deliver it.

"You, come here," Bunin leaned from the office and beckoned.

Paul shivered and his stomach suddenly complained noisily. He straightened his back, however, and walked over to the office.

"Right," Bunin sat down behind the desk. "Shut the door."

Paul did so, then looked for a chair. There was not one on his side of the desk, so he had to stand. He clasped his hands behind his back and rocked from one foot to the other.

"Where were you last night?" Bunin demanded.

"I went to London," Paul raised his chin.

"I hope you enjoyed yourself."

"Yes, thank you."

"Good, because that is what you will be doing most nights from now on."

"What?" Paul frowned. A rock barged into his bowels.

"I have decided to give you one more chance. Just one. I do not train you for the money. I certainly do not train you for the fun of it. I train you because I, Grigor Bunin, believe you and Anna to be a competent dance pair. I do not, however, believe you to be an indispensible part of that pair. You are a component, no more. You can be replaced."

"But . . ."

"Last night, you left Anna alone here with nothing to do. You wasted my time and hers. Luckily I was able to find another reasonable skater to take your place."

The blood drained from Paul's face. "Who?" he croaked, then cleared his throat, "Who?"

"A young man named Keevil, not that it concerns you. Now listen. I expect one hundred and fifty per cent from you, Paul. At the moment I am getting only ninety. I fully understand that you are a young man and that the world is full of temptations, but the same temptations will be there in five years' time. What you do affects at least two other people. You have no right to behave so irresponsibly. You know, I think, that I do not make idle threats. I do not change my mind either. You may be stubborn, but I am more so, and I am in the position of power. One more failure to turn up for practice and you are out, do you understand?"

"Yes, but I don't see . . ."

"Splendid," Bunin stood and held out his hand, "we will consider that settled. Anna is already on the ice. You will apologize to her. Good. Thank you, Paul."

Paul shook Bunin's hand almost absently. Bunin picked a sheaf of papers off the desk and flicked through them as though he had forgotten Paul's existence. Paul stood there irresolute. He knew that he had something righteously indignant to say but he could not remember quite what it was. He felt that he was the victim of injustice, but Bunin appeared to have anticipated his every argument. He trembled with anger and frustration. His fists opened and closed at his sides. At last he exhaled with a hiss and turned away.

"And, Paul . . ." Bunin said behind him.

"Yes?"

"Please shut the door gently."

A sort of growl forced its way up from Paul's stomach, but he closed the door very quietly behind him. Then he kicked the wall.

Six months it took. Six months that restored the old blisters on Paul's feet and turned them into permanent callouses harder than shoe-leather. Six months that saw Anna grow more than an inch and saw both of them becoming more and more expert and unified as a pair. Six months of rancour, bitterness and constant hard work.

Paul put up with Steve's good natured taunting. Anna put up with the endless battle between Paul and Bunin. It was not an open battle. Paul turned up on time and worked as hard as she, but although the young buck had been given a sharp lesson by the old stag, he knew, as did Bunin, that confrontation must come again. Paul was tense, aggressive, impatient. He did not laugh at Bunin's occasional jokes but sneered and urged, "Let's get on with it" all the time. At home, too, he was moody and spent most of his time alone in his room.

It was not that Paul chose to behave thus or even liked himself for doing so. It was just that he felt torn apart by two sides of his nature. On the one hand, he wanted to skate and saw, in his more charitable moments, the reasons for which Bunin was stern and unbending. On the other, he wanted to scoff at Bunin's high seriousness, to assert himself and to have a normal life. The battle that had for so long been fought between his parents now raged in him. He yearned too, as ever, for solitude, but when he was not at school he was skating. There was no time in which to be alone.

On the first day of the summer holidays, Anna fell heavily on her left knee. She was still limping a week later. The doctor said something about loose splinters of bone in the fluid on her kneecap. He ordered two weeks' rest. Gabriella took advantage of the break to take Anna home to Italy for a brief holiday.

"Let's all take a breather," Bunin suggested. "Paul. I want you to keep in practice with – what? Three hours a day? Just do a few figures and keep in shape, OK?"

"Yeah, OK. Here or at Richmond?"

"Wherever you like. I won't be there. I'm going to have

a bit of a holiday too. We meet up two weeks from today, first thing in the morning."

Paul rang Steve as soon as he got home that evening. "Hey, great!" Steve cried. "Hang on a second while I turn down the music, OK, mate?"

Paul listened to some distant banging and crashing. "Right, now," Steve returned, "tell us the news, mate."

"I've got two weeks off!" Paul announced.

"What?"

"I've got no skating for two weeks. I was wondering if we could meet up."

"Well gee whiz, wow and yeehah. Two weeks of real life. I regard it as my sacred duty to fill every hour of every day with evil-doing. Tell you what, you got some cash?"

"Yup. Haven't had anything to spend it on for six months."

"Great. Well look, why don't you come up and doss down 'ere for a bit? No point in getting trains 'ither and yon, is there?"

"I don't know . . ." Paul hesitated, then, "OK, yeah, I'd love to. Sure it's all right with your parents?"

"Oh, my mum won't mind. She's laid back about things like that. No probs. She's hardly ever 'ere anyhow. All you 'ave to do is pack up a bag, empty your piggy bank and it'll be wine, women and song for the next two weeks. What say you?"

Paul took a deep breath. "Sounds great," he grinned. "We'll blow the town apart."

Steve lived in an elegant Georgian red-brick crescent overlooking gardens in Stockwell. The sunlight was heavy on Paul's shoulders as he lugged his overnight bag up the steps to the front door.

It opened just as he raised his hand to the bell. A tall, fat woman with long blonde hair stood in thc doorway. She wore a long kaftan of orange, yellow, white and black. A huge square yellow ring flashed on her right hand. The flesh of her feet bulged out through the straps of golden sandals. "Hi!" she squealed. "You must be Paul! Great. I'm Bunty, Steve's mother. Good to see you. I'm just off. You'll find Steve upstairs somewhere. Hope I'll see you before you go. Byeee!"

She swept past. A warm cloud of scent followed her like a dog at heel. Paul looked after her with a gormless, polite smile on his face.

"Paul!" Steve's voice called from indoors. "Hi. Come on up."

Paul shut the front door. He was standing in a large living room. The walls were covered with some sort of canvas the colour of wet sand and adorned with large, colourful abstract paintings. There were dried flowers in a cauldron in the grate. The two tables were very low and of lacquer. There were lacquer cupboards and screens too. At the far end, large windows overlooked the garden.

Paul laid down his case and trotted up the stairs. "Where are you?" he called. On either side of the landing the doors were open. There was an office, two bedrooms and an opulent bathroom with purple walls, a large Victorian bath and rubber-plants on heavy mahogany stands.

"Up here!" Paul ran up the further flight of stairs and pushed open the door on his right.

"Hi, mate, good to see you." Steve lay sprawled on a bed at the other end of a high attic room with sloping pine-plank walls. There was a full sized ping-pong table at the centre of the room. The walls were lined with baggy red armchairs and sofas. Two girls also looked up as Paul entered. One sat at the foot of the bed. She was slightly plump. She had short auburn hair. She smiled and said "Hi."

"This is Nicky," Steve touched her arm, "and that, over there, is Karen."

The girl that he indicated was perhaps sixteen. She was kneeling on the rug flicking through a magazine. Her hair was shoulder length, straight and golden. She flicked it aside to say "Hello". She had very bright grey-green eyes. She did not smile. Her lips turned down at the corners. She looked casual, almost bored. She wore a smocked white cotton shirt and tight faded jeans.

"Grab yourself a beer from the 'fridge and sit yourself down." Steve stretched. "Boy, have we got a programme for you."

"Oh, yeah?" Paul reached into the little 'fridge. He pulled out a can of lager and ripped off the ring-pull. "So, what's in store? Tell me all about it." He sank into the armchair overlooking Karen and took a swig from the can.

"Well, tonight I thought we'd go clubbing a bit, grab some dinner down King's Road or something. Tomorrow there's the Springsteen concert, for which, you will be delighted to know, we have tickets, though you've got to give Karen the cash for yours and hers, then Thursday I thought we'd get a few bottles in and have a party here. Friday, I think Nicky and I have got a party, but you can do what you like, then Saturday . . ."

"Hold up," Paul laughed, "I'm going to be a physical wreck after this lot."

"Nah," Steve lit two cigarettes and handed one to Nicky, "You're an athlete, mate. More stamina than the rest of us put together."

"Yeah, well. I'm still meant to be skating a few hours in the mornings."

"Oh, leave it out!" Steve groaned. "This is meant to be a holiday, my old son. We drink, we party, we sleep. I mean, you wouldn't believe how many hours this guy skates every day. What is it, Paul, six, seven?"

"Seven, sometimes eight," Paul shrugged.

"Hell," Nicky puffed smoke through her nostrils, "must be a masochist."

"You get used to it."

"Yeah, well, not here you don't, kiddo." Steve swung his legs from the bed.

"I'd quite like to see this famous skating," said Karen.

"Yeah, so would I," Nicky nodded. "Sounds good. Good for a laugh, anyhow."

"Now look what you've started, Paul. For God's sake! OK, so one day perhaps we go down the rink and watch him skidding, but one day, right? Not every morning."

"OK," Paul agreed wryly. "Now," he turned to the girl beneath him. "Where are you from, Karen?"

Paul got very happily drunk that night. After dinner at an American hamburger joint in the Fulham Road, they took a taxi to Campden Palais, where the throbbing barrage of the bass made Paul feel that his heart had stopped. For all his experience of ice dance, Paul knew nothing of disco dancing. Karen laughed at him and gave him a lesson, encouraging him to abandon his inhibitions and giggling at his inability to do so. Gradually, however, the music, the heat and the wine made him relax and, after midnight, he found her dancing in his arms. When they returned to Stockwell at a quarter to two, Steve and Nicky kissed on the sofa while Paul and Karen, slightly embarrassed, played table-tennis. It was after four when the girls at last telephoned for a taxi home.

The following day, Paul awoke and leaped from his bed in a panic before he realized that he was at Steve's house. He looked at the alarm clock by the bed. He picked it up and listened to it. He looked at his watch. He picked it up and shook it. Only then did he believe that it really was half-past eleven. It had been many years since he had got up so late.

He was to get up so late every day for the next fortnight.

That night at Wembley, Paul bopped in the aisles with the best of them as Springsteen growled and groaned and yelled. They met some acquaintances of Steve's at the concert and ended up in a basement flat in Battersea with a few litres of red wine, three cats, a huge bowl of spaghetti and a lot of people whom Paul had never seen before. He lay sleepily with his head in Karen's lap and she tried to pour wine into his mouth. A lot of it splashed over his chin and his shirt front. Paul just giggled.

"Well, mate," Steve said on the third night. He fastened his gold cufflinks and studied his reflection in the mirror, "You're on your own tonight. I trust you to behave entirely dishonourably in my absence. Help yourself to booze and things. You never know," he smirked and ran his finger round his collar, "you could be in for a cosy little night with mam'selle Karen. She likes you. You can see that. Go to it, lad."

"Shut up," Paul grinned.

"No, I mean it! Why not? Make the most of it, I say. Never waste an opportunity. Remember, it's back to Kindergarten for you in a week's time."

Steve and Nicky had already left when Karen arrived in jeans and a sparkling tee-shirt. "Hi," she said. That was all. No smile, no warmth, just that usual weary tone. She slumped into a chair. Steve's suggestions had had their effect. Paul could not help observing the slick of gold light on her forearms, the small pointed breasts beneath the white cotton as she reached up to take the drink that he brought her.

"What'd you like to do, then?" Paul asked.

She shrugged. "Dunno. What do you fancy?"

"Hungry?"

"Bit, I suppose."

"Chinese, Italian, French, Indian?"

"Dunno. Chinese."

"OK, Chinese it is. Look, it's a great evening and I'm half dead after last night. Let's have a quiet evening. It's beautiful out there. We could have a stroll, get something to eat then come back here and . . ."

"Yeah. Suits me."

"Great," he sat on the arm of the chair. Her hair touched his naked forearm. He raised his hand and lightly stroked it. She did not move away. If anything, he thought, she leaned a little towards him. "Know any good Chinese places?" he murmured casually.

His hand stroked the nape of her neck. Her skin was very warm. Now she definitely leaned back. "Mmm," she sighed. "That's nice. Nope. We can look one up. Must be one in the area."

"Yup, OK," Paul's thumb caressed the lobe of her left ear. "Where did you get these, then?" He touched the delicate enamel butterfly earrings.

"My mum," she said. "Got them in Eyetieland. Like 'em?"

"Yeah. Not bad."

Her right hand arose lightly to hold his arm. Her head turned up towards him. Her bright eyes flashed up at him.

"Right," she said briskly, "you ready to go?"

"Yup," Paul smiled. He took the opportunity to lean forward and quickly to kiss her lips. "Let's be off."

They walked in Hyde Park and again Paul contrived to put his arm around her waist and to kiss her a couple of times. They ate in Soho and Paul asked Karen a lot of questions about herself and her family. She answered with her usual laconic, blasé air, but her eyes sparkled a lot in the candlelight and, although two days ago Paul had found her fairly pretty but no more, now he discovered, to his astonishment, that she was beautiful. She slapped his hand in reproof, touched his arm to get his attention. That barrier had been broken.

"See you tomorrow?" Paul asked more eagerly than he had intended.

"Maybe," she replied coolly, "give us a bell."

Suddenly she spoke confidently, even arrogantly. There was a new assurance in the manner in which she swung back her shoulder-bag and blew a kiss from the open door. She had got him and she knew it.

He was in love.

"Dear Paul," Anna wrote from the beach at Porto Ercole, "The sun is shining, the sea is warm, the knee is better and I am tanned and stunningly beautiful. Gabi cannot understand how I can possibly miss a block of ice in the middle of rainy London, but I do. I am evidently going mad. I miss Streatham and you and even being shouted at by Mr Bunin. Tomorrow we return to Padova and the grandparents. See you on Monday. Gabi sends much love. Anna."

The postcard was delivered to the Crispins' house on the second Thursday of the fortnight, just three days before the Lombardis returned.

Paul did not return home to find it until the following Wednesday.

"But *why*?" Anna sobbed. She sucked up a deep tritone breath, "Why, why, why, why, why?" The last word ended in a little whipcrack whimper. She shook her head and stared miserably down at her hands on the kitchen table. She made no effort now to hide the tears or the redness of her eyes. Her shoulders shook as she struggled to regain breath. "I – I mean, we've put so much into it. All that work, all that time . . ."

"I know, darling," Gabriella leaned forward and stroked her daughter's hair. "I know."

"And you! All the scrubbing and cleaning and long hours . . . I mean, how can he do this to us?"

"I don't know. I think he's been under a lot of pressure from his family and things. And boys of that age – well, they have problems. It's very important to them to look like men."

"And this makes him look like a man, does it?" Anna snarled, "Running away from obligations, deserting people who've been good to him, abandoning responsibility? Is that how the English see a man?"

"Some of them, I'm afraid," Gabriella sighed, "yes."

"Well, they are pathetic. I spit on the English and their precious manhood."

"Paul is a boy." Gabriella spoke calmly. "He is just trying to be a man, and he doesn't understand what it means. It is pathetic."

"What did his mother say?" Anna looked up at the strip light. Her lower lip trembled.

"She doesn't understand either. She can't get him to listen or see sense. She has tried, but he's at a difficult age. He is rude and won't listen. He has made some bad friends at his school."

"Do you think – can you make him listen?"

"I can try," Gabriella shrugged, "but I doubt that it will work. I doubt that he would even talk to me. He's got to work it out for himself."

"But it will be too late!" Anna wailed. "We have just two months until the Juniors. And even if he did come back, Mr Bunin wouldn't train him any more."

"You cannot blame him. He too has put a lot of time and effort into training you. If Paul is going to disappear like this at a moment's notice, why should he bother? But I have talked to him. He has not said 'never'. If Paul ever grew up enough to say 'sorry' and to mean it . . ."

"I would not skate with him," Anna said with sudden defiance.

"Then you would be stupid too. Everyone must learn their lessons. Everyone must try things out. The important thing, as an ancient Greek philosopher said, is not that someone enters a place of sin and silliness, it is whether they ever come out. Perhaps Paul is one of those sad people who never come out, who get hooked like an addict on worthless things. Perhaps on the other hand he tries it and so gets rid of the bad thing that is in his blood. He will know then that it is not worth it and will be able to return to real life without always hankering for something else. Anyhow, you can't worry about that. You must look to the future for now. Osbert is a good skater. He has his Silver like Paul . . ."

"He is not as good as Paul."

"No, but he is a worker . . ."

"And I don't like him as much as Paul."

"I thought you hated Paul."

"I do!" The tears came again. Anna hit the table again

and again as she struggled to master them. "But he is a child, Mama," she croaked, "a stupid, stupid child."

Gabriella smiled in recognition. "True," she said softly, "and you may be two years younger, but in many ways you are much older and wiser, so you know that you cannot hate him. It is stupid and pointless. One day, who knows? He may grow up and you can be friends. In the meantime, please remember, I invested all my time and money in you, not in Paul and you. It has been time and money well spent and I do not regret a minute or a penny, but if you throw it all away now, I shall. You must work ten times as hard now to teach Osbert. Forget about Paul."

"All right," Anna nodded and sniffed, "All right. He doesn't exist. He never existed. Paul Crispin," she announced like a Hollywood empress, "is dead."

Paul Crispin sat by the stream and threw twigs into the water. He could not think of anything else to do until this evening when he was to meet Karen. Ever since he had returned home, he had spent his mornings in bed, his afternoons, when he could not meet Steve, down here at the bottom of the garden and his evenings in town with Karen or with Steve. He did not want to talk to anyone else. His mother wished to accuse him. Katie just wanted to crow. His father showed embarrassing concern.

Paul needed no accusations. Already a large part of him regretted the rebelliousness which had made him give up a friendship and a way of life. He missed the regular practice sessions, the sense of purpose when he woke up every morning. He was drifting now in no particular direction. He had just one end, one purpose left in his life.

Karen.

He had not been able to reconcile the two warring factions in his life, so he had had to choose. He was committed now to the faction which Steve, Karen and their friends represented. He had kicked off the restrictions of childhood. He was no longer a mother's boy. He had elected to grow up and to join the world of men.

In the world of men, however, there were problems. Of these, money was the most immediate. Those two weeks with Steve had cleaned out his current account and his mother still had control of his deposit account and despite his protests, would not yield it. His allowance came in once a month, but high standards had been set in those early days when Paul had had apparently limitless funds. Karen was used to dining out, to concerts, to discos, and Paul had no home in London to which he could take her for quiet evenings.

At the beginning of August, he had spent his £100 allowance in the space of eight days. Since then, he had sold his silver christening mug, his old stamp collection and a gold watch chain with a spade-guinea fob which his grandfather had left to him. Now, on August 24th, he had just ten pounds in his pocket. Still worse, Steve's house, his one refuge in London, was locked up. Bunty McCall and her lover had taken Steve off on a two week holiday in Ibiza. Mrs Crispin had been willing enough to fork out for skating expenses, but she had proved surprisingly stubborn about providing money for Paul's unexplained trips to London.

"Paul?"

He started. His mother's voice was very near. He had not heard her approach. She stood on the other side of the stream. Her eyes were so full of puzzled perturbation that Paul wanted to hit her. Or himself. He looked away from her.

"Paul, I want to talk to you," she said. "It's no good ignoring me or trying to run away. You can't run away forever, you know."

"What is it?" he said dully.

"I've just received a call from Mrs Lombardi."

"Oh, yes?"

"Yes, and she is as mystified as I am about this whole business. Anna is apparently deeply distressed and frankly I don't blame her. You can't just run out on people like this."

"I just did."

Mrs Crispin muttered a prayer under her breath. "Yes, we know that you did," she said, "and it's a way I'd have hoped no son of mine would have behaved. And ever since, you've been impossibly bloody to everyone. You're sulky, rude and thoroughly unpleasant. You give absolutely nothing to the family or to anyone, and I'm fed up." She sat on her hunkers and plucked up clumps of grass. "What is it, Paul?" she pleaded. "Something's bothering you. That's obvious."

"Nope," he said casually. "Nothing's bothering me. Seems something's bothering everyone else. They just can't leave me alone."

"No one's trying to pester you, Paul," June Crispin soothed. "It's just – you're making life hell for a lot of people, you know. You've created an unhappy atmosphere for everyone here. I mean, your father was saying that he's beginning to dread coming home at night. Katie's having a horrible time. I'm having a horrible time, and as for Anna and Mr Bunin . . ."

"Bunin was paid," Paul snapped. "If I decide I don't want to go on, that's my business. It's nothing to do with him."

"That's absolute nonsense, Paul and you know it." Mrs

Crispin struggled to control the angry quavering of her voice. "Mr Bunin was paid because he has to live, but he's not just any old professional teacher, you know. I mean, top actors get paid too, but they still accept or reject parts. It's not just a matter of anyone who gives them the cash getting their services."

"I don't care how good he is," Paul sneered, "He's an egomaniac."

"He has more right than some people I could name," said June Crispin drily, "and much better manners. Now listen, Paul, please. Tell me what's wrong and we'll try to sort it out, whatever it is."

"It's nothing."

"Is it a girl? Is that it?"

"It's nothing," Paul's voice rose, "I've told you!"

"All right," Mrs Crispin stood with a sigh, "but I am deeply ashamed to see my son behaving like a spoiled, ill-mannered, inconsiderate little brat. I really admired the courage that you showed in your skating. I was proud of the way you fought against all the pressures and came out on top. I supported you against your father and your teachers . . . You showed guts and character. But now," her voice faltered. Paul could hear that she was crying. He could not turn and look. "Now you're proving yourself to be nothing but a cowardly slob. We're all heartily sick of you, do you understand? Sick and tired of you!"

Her voice receded, then there were just two ever quieter little sobs as she walked back up the garden to the house. Paul lay casually on one elbow and shook his head knowingly. Only when he was certain that he could no longer be seen did he lay his head down in the cool grass, screw up his eyes and open his mouth wide in a silent scream.

* * *

"It's not as easy as it looks, this dancing business," Osbert Keevil stirred his coffee. His forehead and his dark curly hair were pearled with sweat. It was six o'clock. They had been skating for just one hour. Bunin was due to arrive for the second training session of the day in just a few minutes.

"I know," Anna laughed. "That's because it's boring. I mean, anyone can sort of fling themselves into big jumps or whatever, and that feels great because it's exciting and immediate, you know? Great opportunity to show off, dancing. It's all tiny things. Just minute alterations in steps and hand movements to get the tracings and the lines absolutely perfect, and then, when you've got it right, going over it again and again and again until you can do it in your sleep. It's great when it all works on the day though."

"Yes, yes, I can see that," Osbert showed his teeth. "And you look wonderful when you're dancing." He licked his lips, "I could eat you all up," he enunciated perfectly.

Anna suppressed a shudder. "Yes, well," she said, "we'd better be getting back."

"Hold on a mo," Osbert's hand grasped hers. For all the sweat on his brow, his hand was soft and dry as doeskin, "I was wondering, doll. How about you and me going out one evening, have a nice quiet dinner somewhere? We never seem to talk about anything except blessed skating. We could get to know each other better."

"I don't think so," Anna smiled sweetly. "We're busy every evening anyhow."

"Well, there's always Sunday."

"It's the only day I get a chance to wash my hair and collapse in front of the television."

"*Please*." He somehow contrived to turn it into a four syllable word.

"Well, we'll see," said Anna briskly. "Look, there's Mr Bunin. We'd better be getting back to the rink. Come along, now."

Paul ran from the bus to the Picasso café, dodging the passers-by. He was out of breath and his hair flopped over his eyes as he pushed open the door and looked around the room for Karen. He was ten minutes late.

"Hi, Paul." Karen spoke from the table behind him. He swung round, smiling.

"Hi, Paul," said Nicky. She gave a little giggle like water going down the plug.

Paul looked quickly from one girl to the other. The frown appeared on his face and vanished in a split second, like fingers sweeping over harpstrings. "Hello," he smiled. "Nice to see you, Nicky." He pulled out a chair and sat.

"Yeah, well," Karen droned, "I asked her to come along."

"Sure!" Paul waved, "Sure, it's fine."

"So," Nicky exchanged a quick glance with Karen, "what's the plan for tonight, Paul?"

"Well . . ." Paul hesitated, "I'm a bit cash-free at the moment. We could do a movie or something."

"Yeah, OK," Karen yawned. "We'd like to see the new Tom Cruise."

"OK." Paul shrugged. "If that's what you want."

"Karen's been telling me about all that you two have been doing," Nicky drew on her cigarette with a little "pht". "Sounds as if you've been having a good time."

"Yeah, we've been getting around, haven't we, Karen?" Paul did his best imitation of Steve.

"Sort of." Again Nicky and Karen exchanged that rapid

glance. "Tell you what, Paul. Why don't you go and get a *Standard* so's we can see what time the film starts?"

"OK," Paul sighed. "Yup. Right. Won't be a second."

He threw a quick look of anger and frustration at Karen as he walked back to the door. She did not even see it.

Throughout the film, Paul sat straight-backed and seethed. Once he put his hand on Karen's knee only to have it brushed off. Once he put his arm around her shoulder. She instantly leaned forward, apparently to offer a sweet to Nicky who sat on her right. The two girls talked to one another from time to time. Paul passed a couple of remarks to Karen. She merely said "yes" to each of them and never looked away from the screen.

"Come and have a drink," Paul said afterwards.

"No, don't bother, Paul," Karen said stiffly.

Nicky smiled. "No. Seeing as you're a bit short of the ready . . ."

"Not that short." Paul insisted, "Come on. Please. I've hardly had a chance to talk to you."

Again that glance, then, "OK, but just one, then we must be going home."

At the pub, Paul decided to let his anger show. He banged the drinks down on the table and took no part in the conversation save to agree irritably with everything that was said. Once he mouthed "I want to talk to you" to Karen. She looked away with a deep sigh.

At last, Nicky announced that she "must go to the khasi."

"So," Paul leaned forward as soon as she was out of earshot, "what's all this about?"

"All what?" Karen looked vaguely surprised.

"Bringing Nicky along. I mean, there's nothing wrong with Nicky, but I haven't had a word or a . . . We haven't had a chance to be together all evening."

"What are you talking about? We've been together. Just had my best friend with us, that's all. Steve's out of town, so . . ."

"Yes, I know, but I'd like to talk to you."

"Well, we're talking."

"No. Properly. I mean talk properly."

"Nothing much to talk about really, all you can do is sulk."

Paul nodded. "OK," he said. "I'm sorry. It's just – well, naturally I want to be alone with you. You know that."

"I can't really see the point." She tipped peanuts into her palm and slapped them into her mouth.

"What do you mean, can't see the point?"

"Well, you know. You and me." Karen munched. She looked unconcerned. "I mean, it can't go anywhere. Shouldn't have let you get involved in the first place really, but you know, it was fun. Nothing else to do. Didn't expect you to – well, go overboard like you did."

"I didn't go overboard," Paul's voice became a sort of husky squeak, "I mean . . ."

"Look, Paul," Karen rocked her head from side to side. "You're just too heavy about things. I mean, I like you, right, so we have some fun together, but it's nothing more'n that. Just a bit of a laugh."

"A bit of a laugh?" Something seemed to burst and spread in Paul's brain like a slow-motion film of an atom-bomb. "Look, I love you, Karen. I mean, the things we did and said and . . ." He gasped. His chest was suddenly constricted.

"So, sure," Karen nodded, "We mess about a bit, dance a bit, what's so odd about that? But you don't love me, Paul," she cackled. "And I don't really fancy you. Nothing personal, but there you are. So you see, I mean, there's no future in it, is there? No point in seeing one another."

"But Karen, for God's sake . . ."

"Oh, come on, Paul," Karen grinned and touched his knee. "Stop being heavy about this. That's the whole problem, isn't it? I like guys who can make me laugh, just have a good time, you know? And you want to lay all this deep stuff on me. I mean, life's too short, you know? Sorry, Paul, but that's it. Hi, Nicky." She looked up, picked up her bag and stood.

"Ready to go?" Nicky cooed.

"Yup."

"See you, Paul. Thanks for the movie."

"Yeah, thanks, Paul," Karen turned at the door and waggled her fingers at him. "See you round."

Paul stood and stared at the door as it swung slowly shut. He sank back on to the low stool. Karen's every word seemed to echo simultaneously in his mind in one vast discord. A little sob forced its way up from within him and escaped like a bubble from his lips. He tensed every muscle in his body until he trembled. A wavering screen of black seemed to push down over his eyes. He wanted to hit someone. He wanted to cry.

He drained his pint and the girls' half-full glasses and examined the change in his hand. He had just thirty-six pence left. Not enough for a drink. "She can't . . ." He forced the words out as he stood. "She can't, she can't, she *can't*."

He flung the door open and stumbled out into the street. A sports car howled past. His brain was cold and numb. Tears would not come, though a string of vile names sprang to his lips as he walked back to the bus-stop, noticing nothing.

Suddenly, he realized, he was more alone than ever before in his life.

Anna never knew why she let it happen. Curiosity, perhaps, or mere apathy, laziness or disillusionment.

It was after her first competition with Osbert. They had come tenth. Anna would have welcomed a good performance. She would have tolerated a disastrous performance. This however was that least tolerable of things; messy, moderate, inept. Osbert beamed at the audience and did everything just about right. He did nothing, however, with precision or with gusto. He took no risks. He was irritatingly slow and flamboyant in his every action, like an ingratiating waiter or an actor playing second courtier and hoping to be noticed. Anna tried to push things along and, by doing so, made things still worse.

As they came off the ice, they were met by Cliff Owen and Sandra Bailey. "Hello, Anna." Sandra smiled like somebody's mother, "That was very nice."

"Thanks."

"I can't think why you didn't do better. That's always been such a successful free dance in the past."

"Yes, well. We're adapting. It's a new partnership."

"Yes, it takes time." Cliff nodded sagely, "Took us four years, didn't it? Of course, we were twelve and fourteen."

"Yes," Sandra gushed, "but I think it's really brave of you. Really. Starting at this age. But this time, Anna, honestly, you must hold on to your partner. You can't change too often without getting a bad name. Know what I mean? Especially for a girl. Looks bad."

Anna grinned in such a way that the sound "Hng" came from her throat.

"Four years!" Osbert followed her to the changing-rooms. "Four years! God! I mean, I'll be twenty-one by then and I'll have to be in the seniors and they – they've been at it four years and are still only at the top of the juniors."

"Yup, it's a long way," Anna said flatly, "I thought you knew that." She sat and started to unlace her boots.

Osbert gulped. He nodded. "Oh, yes, yes. 'Course. Just a bit of a shock when you think about it, that's all."

Anna somehow summoned a weary encouraging smile. This sort of talk must be discouraged. That one smile was enough for Osbert. His mouth bunched and uncurled like a caterpillar walking across his face. "How about that dinner, then?" he purred. "Cheer us up a bit, eh? Just something quiet, you know. Anyhow, it's Sunday tomorrow."

Anna was drained and depressed. If he had asked her to jump off a cliff with him at that moment, she would not have had the energy to say "no".

She sat through dinner more or less in silence. The food was supposed to be Italian. Occasionally Anna nodded or faintly smiled. That was all that was needed. Osbert liked the sound of his own voice. He sang her praises, spoke of famous romantic partnerships and talked of their future association on and off the ice as though it were a foregone conclusion. His conversation veered always towards sex and as suddenly veered away with giggles and wriggles and smirks to underline his true meaning. Had he spoken openly, Anna might not have minded so much.

Once Osbert even so far forgot himself as to explain to her the difference between *penne*, *tagliatelle* and *macheroni*. Anna paid no attention. She was tired. She saw little hope now of attaining the sort of triumphs of which she had dreamed only weeks before. She wanted Paul back.

Prim, precise, perpendicular Paul. If he had walked into the restaurant at that moment, she thought . . . She smiled. She would have done her best to tear his throat out. Then kissed him.

Osbert walked her home, his arm cast casually around her shoulders. She could not object to that. He held her in his arms, after all, for many hours of the average day. At the Robilliard Estate, however, almost as if he responded to a schedule – "Reach Robilliard Estate. Become passionate," – his tone and his manner changed. "Oh, Anna," he breathed, and suddenly the whites of his eyes, lit by a passing taxi, grew nearer and the smell of after-shave was strong and she was pressed up against the wire-netting of the fence, his thin lips working on hers.

She submitted patiently. There was no point, after all, in having a row. There was no point in anything much. His mouth tasted of mint, and she realized with revulsion that he must have used some sort of breath-freshener as they walked.

It lasted perhaps for a minute, perhaps for two, then his hand started to move up her left thigh. She pushed him away and sidestepped from his grip. "Good night, Osbert," she said dully. She wiped her mouth on her sleeve.

"Night, darlin'," his husky voice behind her was eager and joyful. She knew then that she had made a mistake.

"'Ear Karen gave you the push, then?" Steve followed Paul out of the gates of the school. Paul said nothing. "Not to worry, mate. Plenty more where she came from. Get you fixed up in no time. I got rid of that Nicky too, matter of fact. Getting all serious, she was. Still. Plenty more out there."

"S'pose so." Paul smiled glumly.

"Where you off to, then?" Steve asked almost as though he was desperate to please.

"Down Sloane Street. Promised I'd pick up some things for my mother."

"Who's a good little boy, then? Mind if I come with you?"

"No. Fine," Paul sighed. "I won't be staying long though. Got to get back."

"Not skating again are you?" Steve laughed.

"Bit." Paul shrugged. He had been down to Richmond seven or eight times in the past two weeks, once more seeking on the ice the solitude of concentration and the outlet of exercise. He had not told his mother for fear of her approval. "No, but we've got this dinner-party at home tonight. I'm expected to be there."

"Bo-ring!" Steve chanted. "Look, you and I must get together again, have a few nights on the town. It was fun, wasn't it?"

"Yeah, s'pose so."

"Course it was. Never seen a guy so transformed by a few days of living it up. You loosened up, became a whole different person. Can't let you go back into your shell again, can we?"

They caught the tube to Sloane Square. Again, as so often, Paul found himself looking for Anna, as much in apprehension as in hope. He had caught sight of her once when he had been walking by chance in the streets by Streatham Ice Rink. She had not noticed him and he had not dared to approach her.

Paul found cheeses and patés already wrapped and ready for collection in the food hall of the Sloane Street department store. He was about to go upstairs to pick up his mother's new dress when Steve called him over. "Just come with me for a little stroll, mate," he said.

"All right." Paul picked up the two carrier-bags and walked by Steve's side down the aisles of the stationery department and into cosmetics.

"Well, what I always say is, stationery is stationary, wouldn't you say?" Steve frowned as though discussing a serious problem, "I mean, it's still, if you know what I mean. It's not often you see a diary or a postcard going for a run, now is it? Mind you, it could be said that all departments in this emporium are, in the truest sense, stationary departments, couldn't it? I mean, this, now, this cosmetics department, you don't see it doing press-ups or strolling out into the park to pick the daisies, do you?"

"What are you talking about?" Paul frowned, "Look, come on, Steve. They're going to be closed soon."

"True, oh wise one, true. Just a second, mate. Not many brains as quick as yours to get to the nub of things, I must say. Straight to the heart of the problem . . ." Steve reached for a gold box from the shelf on his right and with one smooth movement dropped it into the bag in Paul's right hand. "Walk on," he said out of the corner of his mouth. "Yes, and as you will have read in the works of Confucius . . ."

"No, Steve!" Paul hissed. He glanced anxiously over his shoulders. "Steve," he whispered, "put it back."

"Rubbish," Steve murmured. "Just redistributing wealth. These people are rip-off artists anyhow, the prices they charge. Just balancing things out a bit, that's all. And again," he spoke louder, "you will find it written, 'A lotus-blossom smells not as sweet . . .'"

"Steve, shut up!" Paul snapped as they moved towards the escalator, "we could be arrested for this, for Christ's sakes!"

Steve flapped his arms, and looked over his shoulder,

"Hush up, mate," he said, "No one's seen anything. It's all right."

"It's not damned well all right," Paul was very pale. "It's thieving!"

"So?" Steve shrugged and smiled. "Can't go through life paying for everything, can you? Come on, stop being such a prig, for gawd's sake, Paul. Everybody does it. Let's just get these glad-rags and get out of here." He hopped on to the escalator and laughed down at Paul's angry, frightened face. "Don't worry," he teased, "it'll be *all right.*"

"Not very skilful if it is," the plump man in his grey suit sighed, "but you're right. Better follow them. I dunno. Used to be poor little urchins we were chasing, now it's poor little rich kids with more money in their pockets than we see in a month's wages."

"Yup," said the younger man beside him. His eyes followed Paul and Steve as their legs and feet slowly arose on the escalator and disappeared. "Well, I'll keep an eye on them up there. You stay here. I'll give you the nod on the way down."

He was still just five yards behind Steve and Paul as they came down by the staircase just three minutes later. He looked over to his colleague and nodded once. The plump man pulled himself up and suddenly moved quickly and gracefully towards the door.

"Excuse us," the two men had their hands on the boys' arms before the glass doors had even stopped swinging, "but we have reason to believe that you have in your possession certain goods which you have not paid for. If you would come with us, please."

"Dunno what you're talking about," Steve gave a ghastly grin. "We've just spent a fortune in this store. This young gentleman 'ere 'as been collecting a few things for 'is mum, who's got an account 'ere, 'asn't she, Paul?"

"Oh, for God's sake," Paul groaned, "shut your stupid mouth."

"But, honest, I don't know anything about this, really! You won't find nothing on me."

"Yes, well, we'll sort this out inside, if you please, sir."

"No!" Steve yelped and pulled his arm away. "Why should I come in? I'll sue you for wrongful arrest! I haven't nicked anything and you can't prove I 'ave. I don't believe Paul 'as either, but I certainly 'aven't."

"We do have such things as closed-circuit television cameras, sir." The younger man grasped Steve's arm again. "I'm sure that they will establish who did what. Now, please come along quietly."

Steve looked like something deflated as the import of the words sank in. "Yeah, well," he said desperately, "there may be something as Paul forgot to put down on the account . . . I don't know . . ."

"Steve!" Paul said savagely. Steve's cheeks were very pink, his eyes very wide. He avoided Paul's gaze. "You are a prat," Paul said quietly, "a cheap, second-rate, flashy, cowardly prat, and you make me sick."

Tony Crispin did not speak as he drove down Knightsbridge and the Cromwell Road. Paul sat in the passenger seat beside him and stared down at his own clasped hands. The first words were not spoken until the engine roared as they emerged on the motorway.

"So," Tony Crispin sighed, "what's it all about, old boy?"

"I didn't steal anything, Dad. I promise."

"No, I didn't think you had. That McCall is a very moderate piece of work."

"I know that now."

"And his anxiety to put the blame on you was one of the most shameful exhibitions that I have seen in a long time. No, all right. You're no shoplifter. I accept that. But this is only the last in a series of incidents which have been worrying your mother and me. It's almost as if you've been deliberately mucking everything up – ruining your relationships, making enemies, spending all your cash, moping around the place being bloody-minded to everyone. It all started when you gave up skating."

"But you wanted me to give up skating!"

"I didn't want you to run out on anything. Sure, skating isn't my sport and I was worried about its effect on your work, but that doesn't mean that I wanted you to let everyone down like you did. Matter of fact," his eyes slid sideways. He sounded almost embarrassed. "Matter of fact, I was getting quite proud of you and your skating."

"Yeah?"

"Yes, actually. Now listen, old boy. I know it's a difficult time you're going through. Girls make life hell, lack of girls makes life hell, and you think that it'll take forever to grow up and that prats like McCall have more fun than you, and you're impatient to do everything all at once. But you know, the funny thing is, things somehow always happen at the right time. You don't have to push them. But to me, the McCalls of this world are just playing a pathetic child's game of 'let's pretend'. Only difference is, at your age, it's not sweet, 'cos you can do serious damage, to yourself and to others. See what I mean?"

"Yes," Paul shifted, embarrassed, in his seat.

"Good. Now, the thing is, what can we do to make things easier for you?"

"Dunno." Paul said quietly, "I think I'd like to get back to skating."

"So why don't you?"

"I can't, I'm too old to take up solo again and I've blown it with Anna and Mr Bunin."

"There is such a thing as an apology, you know."

"I'm not apologizing to Bunin. He thinks he's God Almighty."

"I don't think he does," Tony Crispin said casually, "but have it your own way. You'll have to find a new partner and trainer then."

"You can't just *find* an new partner and trainer, Dad."

"Well," Mr Crispin shrugged, "the ball's in your court, son. You sort it out one way or another, but I want it sorted out, understood?"

"Yes, Dad."

"Good. If I have your word on that, we'll say no more about today. Deal?"

Suddenly tears were hot in Paul's eyes. He smiled at his father for the first time in years. "Thanks, Dad," he said tremulously, "it's a deal."

"He is insufferable," Bunin murmured.

Gabriella lay on the sofa, her head in his lap. She smiled up at him. "I know," she said, "Anna comes back steaming with anger every day. I've never seen her so restrained. It's not like her to keep her temper in circumstances like that."

"It is admirable," Bunin admitted, "and probably very good for her. She does it, of course, because she is hoping for a miracle. If she blows up and loses the Weevil, she has no partner. If, on the other hand, a good fairy turns up one day and waves her magic wand, Osbert will turn into the world's greatest dancing partner. She chooses the lesser of two evils. Ha!"

"Has Anna given him any – well, any encouragement?"

"Osbert," pronounced Gabriella, "is the sort of young man who regards a smile and a 'good morning' as proof that you are in love with him. As you say, Anna is nice to him because she needs him, and he instantly assumes that she finds him irresistible."

"He thinks he owns her," Bunin stroked Gabriella's hair. "When she talks to anyone else, he rushes over and preens like a cockerel by her side. Today she fell as I was teaching him. Instantly he rushed to the other side of the rink to pick her up, dust her down, stroke her knee. I said to him, 'Osbert, I was in the middle of a sentence. I expect attention. Anna is perfectly capable of getting up by herself. She has fallen more often than you have had hot dinners.' He said, 'Yes, but one worries so. It is natural, you know, when two people care for one another. I feel – responsible.' I very nearly vomited on to the nice clean ice."

Gabriella giggled. "I know what you mean. He is a dirty, sentimental old man and he is only sixteen. Do you think he is going to be any good – as a partner, I mean?"

"No," said Bunin shortly, "never more than moderate."

"Why did you choose him?"

"Because he is the best available, and I did not want to stop teaching Anna just because of Paul's desertion."

"And?" Gabriella's long lashes arose.

"And?" Bunin said defensively, then relaxed. "All right, yes. I did perhaps have an ulterior motive. If I had stopped teaching Anna, I would have stopped seeing you, and we wouldn't be here now."

"Oh, I think perhaps we would have bumped into one

another on the street quite a lot," Gabriella pressed her cheek against his palm. "It would have happened somehow."

"I think so."

"But what is so sad is that Anna now must carry on with eighths and ninths and tenths because she has a bad – and odious – partner."

"It cannot last," Bunin shook his head. "She will explode one day. I can feel it coming. And if I know Anna's explosions, there will be nothing left but little tiny bits of Weevil scattered all over the rink."

You can get quite attached to a pebble, Paul discovered, when you have kicked it about a bit. This was an ordinary, black sort of pebble of indeterminate shape and insignificant size. Paul had kicked it all the way from school. It had chosen its direction. He had merely followed. It had led him unerringly up to Streatham and now, outside the ice-rink it had developed a bad bout of indecisiveness. It had already gone backwards and forwards up the pavement five times. Paul was going to have to make its mind up for it.

He bent, picked up the pebble and put it carefully in his pocket. There was no point in staying out here in the cold. After all, he was outside a club of which he was a fully paid up member. It was warm in there. True, he did not feel sociable, but, if he was careful, there was no reason why he should bump into anyone that he knew.

He shuddered as he stepped into the foyer and the door hushed behind him. Something cold trickled down his spine. He turned quickly into the dark corridor which led to the upper tiers of seats and the cafeteria. He could hear Bunin's familiar cry below. "No, no, no, no, no!"

He stood at the double doors and looked down at the

rink through the circular windows. The first person that he saw was Bunin, then Anna skated into his field of vision. He had forgotten how graceful she looked on the ice. He had forgotten how high she held her head, how proud was the look on her face. He had forgotten too – perhaps he had never really noticed – how her dark skin seemed to glow against the cloudy white ice.

Bunin took her right hand and in slow motion twirled her round so that her back was to him and his arms around her waist. She turned right, left, right, left, then spun, still holding his right hand, but this time in her left. "Always, always," Bunin had said, "you are tying a knot and unravelling it, making tense and then relaxing. I want almost to hear a sigh of relief from the audience each time it unwinds . . ."

Paul looked down at his hands. He realized that he had been rehearsing the movements of the dance as he watched. He put his hands firmly in his pockets and sighed. His principal feelings were of embarrassment. Here, at the rink, missing what could have been his, he saw the Paul of the past few months as a stranger, an unbelievably foolish and childish stranger who had been petulant, cowardly, impressionable and mean-spirited. He did not like that stranger.

And if he could see and dislike that stranger, how much more must Anna, Gabriella and Bunin? He would never be able to talk to them without seeing in their eyes the emotions that he now felt – despite, dislike and mistrust.

He turned away with a deep breath and whistled quietly as he returned to the foyer. He could not imagine life without an obsession, without the constant impulsion forward which skating had given it over the past four years. He could not imagine being an ordinary person, just living from day to day with no grand dreams to work for, no great giants to tilt at. But that was what he was and what he must be from now on. That in itself was a challenge, as living without a drug must be to an addict, a challenge more dreadful than any other because it went on forever. It stretched out before him like a landscape without landmarks. Living at peace, he realized, was a lot more difficult than living with the pain and the stress, the triumphs and the defeats of war.

Only reflex saved him from being clouted by the big glass door as it swung inward. He started backward and raised a hand. He found himself looking through the half open door at the pinched features of Osbert Keevil. He stepped backward to let Osbert enter. "Hi," he said, and made to get out before the door closed again.

"Oh," Osbert's black eyebrows meshed. "Hello. What are you doing here?"

"I'm a member of this club, as a matter of fact."

"Yes. I know, but – hold on a second. I'd like a quick word."

Paul let the door swing shut. He leaned casually back against it. "Yup?"

"Well, the thing is, Paul, I mean, you caused Anna a lot of distress when you walked out on the partnership, and it's taken a long time for me to get her back on an even keel, you know? And now we're skating together and we're very close and she's happy, and I don't think it's going to do any good for her to see you round. Open old wounds, you know?"

"That's very considerate of you," Paul said politely, "I must say I never saw it as one of my duties as a skating partner to act as Anna's social watchdog. I'll see her if I wish to and she'll see me if she wishes to."

"Ah, but wait. You were just a skating partner, you see?" Osbert spoke as if explaining to an infant, "I am more than that. Anna and I are – well, obviously there are things which, as a gentleman, I cannot reveal, but – we are, as I say, close. Very close. And I think it's only my duty as a result just to ask you, very nicely, not to make life more difficult for her. She doesn't want to see you any more. She's told me that in no uncertain terms. And you're hardly Mr Bunin's favourite person either."

Paul's frown had deepened as Osbert spoke. His fingers had slowly bunched into fists. His heart beat faster and there was surprising warmth in his cheeks. He found it very difficult to stay still or to speak evenly. "Thank you, Keevil," he said quietly, "for your advice. I think I'd better go now before I tear your head off. Good bye."

"Violence never solved anything," Osbert's voice twanged behind him.

"Maybe not," Paul muttered under his breath as he trotted down the steps, "but it sure as hell makes you feel better . . ."

"Paul! Hi!"

He stopped. It was his day for bumping into people. He should never have come. Tracey stood on the pavement in a canary yellow jumpsuit, her hands on her hips. "And where do you think you're going?" she demanded.

"Oh, I was just passing," he mumbled, "I just thought I'd drop in, that's all, see how things were getting on."

"Seriously awfully is the answer. That greaseball can't skate to save his life," Tracey stepped up, threw an arm around his neck and kissed his lips before he was aware of what was happening. She kept her body pressed against his as she went on: "It's really good to see you. Come on. As you're here, you can buy me a coffee."

"Not in there," Paul said quickly.

"Oh, still hiding, are we?" she taunted, "OK, let's go

to the sandwich bar. Come on. I'm not letting you go." She took his hand and pulled him down the street.

"Did you see Annie, then?" she asked over her shoulder as she charged into the café.

"Saw her, yes. Didn't speak to her."

"Twit," Tracey grinned and sat by a table by the window. "Just coffee for me, please, black. And a Kit-Kat. You should have said hello."

"Nah, she's happy enough with slimy Osbert. No point in stirring things up again. Two black coffees, please," he said to the large woman behind the counter, "and a Kit-Kat." Behind him, Tracey hooted.

"So," Paul laid the cups on the table and slid into the bench opposite her, "what's so funny?"

"You are, you berk! Annie happy with the greaseball? You must be kidding! He can't skate and he spends his life pawing her and drooling over her. You know, he's that type. A groper. Yuk."

"But he said – he implied – well, he as good as told me that they were . . ."

"Going out together?" Tracey supplied.

"Well, yeah. He suggested a lot more than that."

"He did *what*?" the laughter left Tracey's eyes. For a second, she looked murderous. "The little *swine*! I'll do him for this if it's the last thing I do. And you believed him, did you? God, you're as bad as he is. Well," she relaxed and smiled. She took Paul's hand and squeezed it. "You're not, actually, but you are a prat. Annie is going barmy with that little twerp hanging about trying to rule her life. She spits on the ground he walks on. So do I, as a matter of fact. What with him drooling too, the carpets are ankle deep in saliva. She's only just polite to him, if that, and that's simply because he's the only partner available. You've got to save her, superman. I mean, God! You should have seen them at Southampton the other day – where I, incidentally, got a stunningly impressive third, not that I wish to crow or anything – I mean, she looked as though she were dancing with a spider! Dancers are meant to look as though they like each other, right? Well, greaseball's idea of liking someone is dribbling all over them and feeling them up, and the audience can see it. All sane human beings shudder at the sight. It's mega-gross and they're asking questions in the House about banning it. Nope. She needs you, Paul."

"'Fraid not," Paul sighed. "She'd like to tear me limb from limb."

"Yes," Tracey said reasonably, "of course she would. Quite right too, but then she'd also like to skate with you."

"And Bunin isn't going to welcome me back with open arms."

"Well, he's not exactly going to beg you, is he? I mean, God, you walked out on him and dropped him in it, didn't you? But I happen to know that he thinks Osbert is something nasty that must have come into the club on his shoe. He's got a number going with Annie's mum, and he likes Annie, so he's doing what he can to keep her skating, that's all. All you have to do is go up to Bunin and say, 'Sorry, I'm a berk, a prat, a twerp, permit me to lick your boots and go to Canterbury on my knees in sackcloth and ashes. Whip me, beat me, mortify my flesh and ooh I'm getting all excited.' That should do for starters," she mused, "all except the last bit."

Even Tracey had to pause to recover her breath after this synopsis. She sipped her coffee. Paul just looked at his as though it had done something to offend him.

"I don't think I could do that," he said at last.

"Oh, yeah? Why not? Too damned proud or something? Leave it out, Paul. You *are* a prat and a twerp for God's sake, so what's the harm in saying so? Annie needs you. You need Annie. Bunin's good for both of you. You've messed things up, so it's up to you to eat humble pie for a while. That's the way the world goes, kiddo." She drank again, then said casually, "Matter of fact, I'd be pretty glad if you came back too. I might spend a bit more time skating."

Paul caught her eye and a grin tugged at his mouth. She smiled back and again her hand covered his. "Come on, Paul," she urged, "for everyone's sake."

"But Bunin's such a heavy," Paul shook his head.

"Bunin is a *trainer*, Paul. Sure, he's tough, but for whose sake? Who's going to get all the glory when you take the Worlds? Not him. A mention somewhere down the column, that's all. It's you that'll be lapping up the lovely money and the adoration of the crowds, isn't it? He knows something about what it takes to be a champion and you know damn all, so he's got to lick you into shape. You've got to give something up in order to get what you want. I doesn't just happen because you're a born genius. In this case, you've got to give up a hell of a lot of pride and independence, but it's for a *reason*, Paul. And anyhow," the tip of her tongue circled her pale pink lips, "You don't have to give everything up, do you?" She looked over her shoulder at the traffic in the street, "Here endeth the sermon," she said, "and I'm meant to be skating, not sitting here talking. I'm off."

She stood and ruffled his hair, then bent and kissed him. His hand ran down her arm as she drew away and turned for the door. Her hand was very warm. Suddenly he grasped it, "Tracey," he said.

"Hmmm?"

"Er, do you think . . . Could you fix it so that I can see

him alone? Without Anna knowing I'm there? Mr Bunin, I mean."

Tracey gaped and laughed, "Well, glory hallelujah!" she cried, "Li'l' ol' Trace has cured the poor afflicted boy! Welcome back to the land of the living, kiddo."

Paul sat in the little office exactly as he had sat there on that Monday morning more than a year ago when his partnership with Anna had first been proposed. He leaned forward, his forearms on his knees, his hands clasped. Nothing in the room had changed. The wastepaper-bin was still full of paper mugs, the desk still covered with papers. The picture of Paul and Anna was still by the filing cabinet where it had always hung, but it had been joined by another, of Osbert and Anna, evidently doing the *Singin' in the Rain* programme – Paul's and Anna's programme.

Paul looked at his watch and sighed. Tracey had left him twelve minutes ago. What the hell was Bunin playing at? Then he corrected himself and grinned ruefully at his own arrogance. Bunin, of course, would come when he felt like it. He was not at Paul's beck and call. If anything, it was the other way around. It was Bunin who had the power to give or take at will and Paul who must submit to his will if he was to attain what he desired.

Footfalls approached outside. Paul straightened. His right hand fluttered nervously over his crown. He took a deep breath. The door opened. Paul jumped to his feet.

Bunin breezed in, said "Hi, Paul," picked up a sheet of paper from the desk and started to read it.

Paul had expected a sombre, formal interview. This casual approach threw him. He could think of nothing to say. Bunin read whatever it was, hummed a little and picked up another sheet of paper.

"Um," Paul said.

"Yup?" Bunin raised his eyebrows.

Paul silently cursed him. Bunin was not helping. Paul was going to have to do all the work. The man was an autocratic sadist.

Again he corrected himself. Again he mocked himself. Why, after all, should Bunin have anything to say to him? It was Paul who had requested the meeting.

"I wanted to say," he started, "I just wanted . . ." He licked his lips and blurted, "I wanted to say that I am really very, very sorry for having failed to turn up for practice and for having let you and Anna down and I've been a prat and a berk and . . . yes, well, I've been incredibly stupid and I'm sorry."

Bunin laid down the paper and sat. "Thank you, Paul," he said simply, "please, sit down."

Paul sat. Bunin swept the papers on the desktop aside and leaned forward. "I agree with everything you say, Paul," he said, "and I am very glad you came, I have been expecting you."

"You . . . ?" Paul frowned.

"Well, let us say I have been hoping. Can I take it, Paul, that you would like to resume training with Anna?"

"Yes," Paul's voice was faint and husky.

"Can I also take it that you have learned your lesson and will not be such a – prat and berk, I think you said – again?"

"Yes."

"Thank God for that!" Bunin suddenly roared and slapped the desktop. "In that case, as far as I am concerned, welcome back. For Anna I cannot speak. She was very hurt."

"I know." Paul nodded.

"Listen," Bunin sighed, "you have wasted a lot of good skating time. You think perhaps I would never forgive you. That I would treat you like dirt because of your – escapade, ha? Then you strut a bit and say, 'I will not say sorry to that man. Who does he think he is? He cannot give me orders. I pay him,' right?"

Paul gave a small embarrassed smile. "Perhaps," he said.

"Well, let me tell you something, Paul. When I was your age, I was revolting. I knew I was good and I wanted everything all at once. I abused my teacher who had made me good. I wanted girls and fame and money. I wanted to go into the senior classes rather than gaining experience in the junior. I sulked. I refused to make an effort. I turned up late for practice. Everyone hated me, and quite right too. And eventually, my teacher said to me, 'Very well, Grigor Grigorievich. You do not want to skate properly – you do not skate at all.' He told all the other teachers, 'Bunin is not permitted to skate.' In Russia one can do these things. It took me three months to realize that skating was my life. It has taken you two. That makes you a more intelligent prat and berk than Grigor Grigorievich Bunin. So. No, I don't blame you, but if ever it happens again, I will blame you terribly, because you will have had the lesson and not learned. Right, now. Go down to the rink. Your skates are here? No? I will lend you some. Say what you must say to Anna and get rid of that Keevil for me. That is your battle." He held out his hand. Paul stood and took it. "Thank you, Paul," Bunin grinned. "Oh, and – good luck."

Tracey circled Anna and Osbert as they waltzed. "D'you tell Anna who you saw on the way in?" she sang.

"No." Osbert snarled at her, "It doesn't concern her. Leave us alone."

"I think it concerns her very much."

"It's got nothing to do with you," Osbert growled, "I sorted it out."

"Just what did you sort out?" Anna demanded. She leaned back against his right arm.

"Oh, it's just – I didn't want you to be distressed, honey. That Paul was hanging about, that's all."

"Paul?" Anna's eyes snapped open, "Here? What did he want?"

"I don't know. I told him that we were quite happy, thank you, and that after all that he had done, no one particularly wanted to see him. Sent him off with a flea in his ear."

"Oh," Anna said sadly, "Yes, well. I wish I'd seen him."

"No, it's better not, sweetheart," Osbert drawled, "I thought it best to send him packing."

"I like to make my own decisions, thank you." Anna said in a controlled, clipped tone.

"What else did you tell him, Ozzie, dear?" Tracey trilled.

"Nothing," Osbert flashed her a look of pure venom. "Keep quiet, will you? We're trying to work."

"You told him that you were having it off with Anna, didn't you, sweetie?"

"Don't be ridiculous," Osbert snapped. He span Anna round faster than the usual tempo of the dance.

"You said what?" Anna squeaked.

"I didn't, lovey, I didn't," Osbert soothed her. "That's just him being malicious. Jealousy. I just told him what I said to you, that we were doing very nicely thank you, and didn't need his sort around." Osbert smiled ingratiatingly.

Suddenly Anna's already stiff body stiffened still more in his arms. Her mouth dropped open.

"What is it?" he asked softly. "Honestly, I didn't say . . ."

There was a tap on his shoulder. He turned.

"My dance, I think," said Paul.

Osbert's arms dropped to his sides, releasing Anna. Astonishment made him look very stupid for a moment, then his mouth twisted and his nose wrinkled in fury and disgust, "I told you . . ." he started.

But Paul paid no attention. He smiled very broadly as he took Anna in his arms and together they set off in a smooth waltz. Tracey giggled and shouted "Ray!"

"I'm very, very, very, very sorry," Paul said quietly.

"Yeah, well," Anna's hands squeezed his. A smile twitched her lips. Her eyes were laughing. "You're going to be a lot sorrier by the time I've finished with you."

"Look, Anna," Osbert skated up and grasped her forearm, "this won't do. Think what he did to you. You're my partner now. It's established. You can just leave us alone, Paul. I'm sorry, but I told you . . ."

"Let go," Paul ordered graciously.

"Anna," Osbert scowled, "really, you can't let him do this. Think of *us*, Anna!"

Anna stopped dancing. She shook off Osbert's hand. She exchanged a brief glance with Paul, then she turned to the little man in black, took a deep breath, and let fly.

Paul had never realized that so many words could be spoken in a minute, but then Anna had been storing them up for a long time. Bunin watched with undisguised delight from the cafeteria as Osbert stalked red-faced from the ice. Even from up there, he had heard every word that Anna had spoken and had found himself agreeing with a large number of them. He returned happily to the office, picked up the telephone and dialled.

"Hello, darling," he grinned, "haven't got a fatted calf in the 'fridge, have you?"

Epilogue.

"They've had it easy of course," Sandra Bailey drawled over her shoulder as the applause at last died.

"Too right," Cliff Owen sniffed, "See that big motor Crispin turned up in? His parents are loaded! Stinking!"

"And that Anna," Sandra nodded her blonde bubbly head, "these Italians, they're not just waiters and ice-cream salesmen these days, you know. Look how she's always dressed. Hardly breadline stuff."

"Too right. That's another thing you've got to bear in mind. The judges give them high marks because she's Italian. They're always biased in favour of foreigners."

"Yeah." Sandra angrily wiped a tear from her right eye and pointed down at the rink, "Look at them. I mean, okay, they were good, but not that good! Look at little Anna playing the star! I bet they paid someone to throw those flowers."

"Sure. They never usually do that at the Juniors. We should know."

"That must be it, surely. They can't come back again."

"They are! They are! God, they're milking it, aren't they?" Cliff jeered. "I mean, OK, so they got the championship, but, I mean, with Bunin behind them . . ."

"They've just had it so easy," Sandra grit her teeth, "so flamin' easy. It's not fair!"

"Don't worry about it, doll." Cliff squeezed her

shoulder. "We're well out of it. They won't have the stamina to make it to the Seniors."

Sandra nodded.

A burly young man in front of her turned and smiled up at her. He wore a striped shirt and a double-breasted suit. His hair was well cut. His cheeks were like plums. He had a broad, slightly silly smile.

"Yuppy twit," thought Sandra, who was not in the mood for Goodwill to all Men.

"Excuse me," said the young man.

"Yeah?"

"Sorry, but my name is Gavin Vane," said Gavin Vane.

"Yes?" said Sandra, suddenly meticulously refined.

"I'd just like to say that graciousness in defeat will do you more good than sour grapes. By the way, I enjoyed your performance."

"Oh." Sandra swallowed a stone.

"And, silly as it may sound to you, we all have problems of one sort or another. I have problems, those two down there have had a sackful of problems. You, it is quite clear, have problems. When you're losing, you like to be working-class and downtrodden. When you're winning, you like to be middle-class and a downtreader. I'm sure you have a considerable future as skaters, but not, I think, as ambassadors for the sport." He grinned especially sweetly and turned back towards the rink.

"By the way," he turned his head again, "I'm sorry. I should declare an interest. I will shortly be related to one of the new champions by marriage. I'm rather exceptionally proud of the fact. Forgive me."

Sandra gulped again.

Gavin Vane's hand was taken and squeezed by the slim dark girl at his left. "Thank you, Gavin," she said, and kissed his cheek.

And Tracey, sitting beneath her, turned and extended her own hand.

"Put it there, Katie Crispin," she said, "nice to be champions, isn't it?"

"Lovely," said Katie.